DRAGONFYRE

DONNA GRANT

D1617626

Praise for
DONNA GRANT

5! Top Pick! "An absolutely must read! From beginning to end, it's an incredible ride."—*Night Owl Romance*

5 Hearts! "I definitely recommend *Dangerous Highlander*, even to skeptics of paranormal romance – you just may fall in love with the MacLeods."—*The Romance Reader*

5 Tombstones! "Another fantastic series that melds the paranormal with the historical life of the Scottish highlander in this arousing and exciting adventure. The men of MacLeod castle are a delicious combination of devoted brother, loyal highlander Lord and demonic God that ooze sex appeal and inspire some very erotic daydreams as they face their faults and accept their fate."—*Bitten By Books*

4 Stars! "Grant creates a vivid picture of Britain centuries after the Celts and Druids tried to expel the Romans, deftly merging magic and history. The result is a wonderfully dark, delightfully well-written tale. Readers will eagerly await the next Dark Sword book." —*Romantic Times BOOKreviews*

"Donna Grant spins a searing and intense tale [that] will keep readers spellbound." —*Romance Reviews Today*

"Highly enjoyable and super sexy."—*The Book Lush*

"Donna Grant's Dark Sword series is slowly climbing to my top three. LOVE IT!" —*Good Choice Reading*

DONNA GRANT

Titles by DONNA GRANT

THE DARK SWORD SERIES
Dangerous Highlander
Forbidden Highlander
Wicked Highlander
Untamed Highlander
Shadow Highlander
Darkest Highlander

THE DARK WARRIOR SERIES
Midnight's Master
Midnight's Lover
Midnight's Seduction
Midnight's Warrior

THE DARK KINGS SERIES
Dark Craving
Night's Awakening
Dawn's Desire

SISTERS OF MAGIC SERIES
Shadow Magic
Echoes of Magic
Dangerous Magic

THE SHIELD SERIES
A Dark Guardian
A Kind of Magic
A Dark Seduction
A Forbidden Temptation
A Warrior's Heart

THE WICKED TREASURE SERIES
Seized by Passion
Enticed by Ecstasy
Captured by Desire

DRUIDS GLEN SERIES
Highland Mist
Highland Nights
Highland Dawn
Highland Fires
Highland Magic
Dragonfyre

STAND ALONE BOOKS
Savage Moon
Mutual Desire
Forever Mine

ANTHOLOGIES
The Pleasure of His Bed
The Mammoth Book of Scottish Romance

Chapter One

Quay of Skulls,
Home of the magnificent blue dragons

"Careful, you idiots," Isran growled. He clenched his hands as he watched the two men slowly carry the heavy, large white egg from the dark depths of the dragon's cave.

He had waited millennia for the chance to take a most prized possession from the revered blue dragons. The egg was worth a fortune, but it wasn't money Isran was after. No, he wanted something far greater than mere coin.

He wanted power.

As a Fae, he felt the pulse of magic in the heart of his realm. Magic was in the sky and the water. It was in the very air he breathed. But it was never, ever enough.

His one taste of black magic had been all it took to show him what awaited him. Since then he had plotted and schemed his way through the ranks of the Fae's most powerful. The few who happened to guess his intentions soon found themselves dead.

Isran's heart thundered in his chest as the egg drew closer. He had a gift for fooling people and gaining their trust. No one had deduced he was the one behind the deaths. Oh, he had been questioned, but by then he had learned to cloak himself, so not even the most powerful Fae had seen what he really was.

He smiled when he thought of the meeting King Theron had called the night before. Theron had wanted his help in finding the killer. It had been all Isran could do not to jump up and down laughing at how easily he had pulled off his quest.

His greatest plot, however, was in the works. By the time he was finished, no one, not even the feared commander of the Fae army, Aimery, would be able to withstand his onslaught of power.

Isran rubbed his hands together and grinned.

One of the men tripped on a loose rock and nearly dropped the egg. Isran cursed under his breath as he glanced at the sky. The men were taking too long, and the dragon would soon return. They had to be gone, or the dragon would slaughter them in an instant.

"Careful," Isran barked. "The egg will be meaningless if you drop it."

Galrar, the brawnier of the two, cut his blue eyes to Isran. "It's damned heavy."

"You don't have much farther."

"Tell me again why you aren't helping?"

Isran clenched his jaw. "If I could have done it myself, believe me I would. I'd much rather work alone."

It had taken Isran years to find the two men before him. The Fae as a general rule did not tolerate any sort of evil and, with the length to which Isran had delved into black magic, he would have been killed on the spot if anyone recognized his wickedness.

Galrar and Mormir had been hiding deep in the northern mountain regions when Isran had sensed them. It hadn't taken much to convince them to aid in his quest, though there was much they didn't know. The lure of coin and the promise of power had swayed them quick enough.

"Easy." Isran held the wicker bedding steady as they rolled the egg inside. He could see all his dreams coming true now that he had the egg.

"By all that's magical," Mormir murmured, a note of fear dripping from his words.

Isran glanced at Mormir before he followed the man's gaze to the sky. The large wings of the dark blue dragon could be seen. The pair of dragons circled above them before one gave an unholy roar and dove at them.

"We need to leave," Galrar screamed.

Isran smiled at his two comrades. "Aye. I do need to leave."

As he disappeared, he could hear their screams mingled with the roars of the dragon.

Chapter Two

Kyndra pulled up on the reins as she reached the stream. She slid from her mount's back and patted the horse's neck, a smile on her face after the exhilarating run. The ride had been brisk and just what she had needed. Kyndra knelt by the water and cupped her hands to bring the cool liquid to her mouth. When she finished, she moved to the giant oak and sat at the base, her back against the trunk.

While her mare drank, Kyndra's gaze followed the long, thick limbs of the oak that branched out above her. Some so heavy they drooped to the ground while their thick foliage shaded her. With the sun high in the sky and a gentle breeze rustling the leaves, she soon found her eyes drifting shut.

The wedding she had attended the previous night had only solidified that she had made the right decision in entering the Dragon Order. She had given her life to the dragons, and she hadn't regretted it once. There were times she got lonely, but being in the Order meant she gave them everything. Seeing her friend give her life and love to her husband was much like what Kyndra had done with the Order. Besides, there wasn't a man in the universe she could imagine wanting to give up everything for.

No man had ever touched her. It was a requirement of the Order. She came to them a maiden, and she had to stay such. It was also a great honor to be in the Order. Few got selected, and for Kyndra it had meant everything

She had known since she was a little girl and watched the magnificent blue dragons that she wanted to be in the Dragon Order. A smile pulled at her lips as she thought back to how excited and fulfilled she had been when she had been given the honor of leading the priestesses of the Blue Order.

Each dragon had their own order, with the high priestess of the entire Dragon Order ruling them all. Kyndra's next step was to become high priestess. Nothing was going to stand in her way either. Everyone knew she would be the next one chosen. She simply had to wait for her time.

Her mare nudged her feet. "Ready to return so soon, Arion?"

Kyndra had dallied long enough. She needed to prepare for the festival tonight. A blue dragon and its mate had laid an egg. It was cause for much celebration, especially since the Blues laid very few eggs. Of all the dragons on the Realm of the Fae, the Blues had more magic than any other. Every death and birth of a Blue was felt throughout the entire realm.

Kyndra rose to her feet and vaulted onto the mare's back. She reached for the reins and was about to turn the horse around when the bone-chilling roar filled the air. She knew that roar. It was a Blue, and the pain and anger that filled the roar left chills racing down her spine.

She slid from the mare's back. "Return home," she told her horse just before she used her magic to transport her to the dragon.

Kyndra opened her eyes to find herself on top of a mountain. The cool air rushed over her, blowing her long hair away from her face. She turned and gasped as one of the Blues lay dead at the entrance to their lair. Next to him were two dead Fae.

"Nay," she whispered, her eyes filling with tears.

The Fae knew how precious all dragons were to their way of life. None would be so foolish as to attack a dragon. She took a step toward the dead dragon, her hand extended. She had to know what or who killed him. The only way to do that was to touch him.

It was a gift the dragon's magic had given the Fae. By being the first to touch a dragon after its death, she would be able to see everything the dragon had seen—and felt—before its death.

Just as she was about to touch the Blue, the ground shook beneath her feet as the female landed next to her mate. Kyndra's heart hammered in her chest.

"I'm here to help."

The female was beyond comprehension though. The pain at losing a mate had crazed her. Kyndra licked her lips, her breath coming faster. She had but one chance to discover the truth. Her hand reached out, the shiny blue scales of the male mere inches from her fingertips.

Another roar rent the air, making Kyndra's ears ring. She covered her ears and stumbled backwards. Her mouth parted in fear as the female leveled her head with Kyndra's. The anger and malice visible in the dark depths of the beast's gaze were enough to halt Kyndra.

"I need to know who did this," she cried. She dropped her hands and took in a steadying breath. It was her duty as leader of the Blue Order to know the dragons. They knew her, every one of them knew her. Why did this one continue to stop her?

"Please," she begged. "Let me help you!"

In response the female opened her mouth and roared as she put herself between her mate and Kyndra. The meaning was clear. Come any closer and Kyndra would die.

Kyndra sighed. "I'm sorry. So very sorry."

She glanced at the dead Fae once more before she transported to the temple of the Dragon Order. She took a deep breath as she gazed down the aisle to the throne and the high priestess. Just as she suspected, every leader of dragons awaited her. Their eyes watched her as she walked toward the throne.

Kyndra had always loved the temple with its floor of white with swirls of blue shot in the marble. Thick columns stood on either side of the vestibule, lining the long walk that led to the throne of the high priestess and the magnificent dome that stood above her.

Many times Kyndra had stared at the glass in the dome memorizing each etching of the story of the melding of dragons and Fae. The temple had always been a place she could come to gather her thoughts. Now, the cold stones seemed to echo the threat of what she had witnessed.

Kyndra's steps didn't falter as she knelt before the high priestess and bowed her head. She had never failed the Order before. It was destroying her that she hadn't been able to talk to the dragon, to make the female understand they needed each other to solve what happened.

"Kyndra."

She lifted her head to stare into the eyes of the high priestess, Julieth. Shame coursed through Kyndra. Never, in all the millennia she had been a priestess had something so catastrophic happened to the order—to *her* dragons.

"Forgive me, Julieth. I have failed the Order."

The high priestess rose from her throne that was made from the same marble. On either side of the throne stood three women, the handmaidens of the high priestess. They never left her side, faithful until their dying breath.

Julieth took Kyndra's hand and pulled her up until they stood face to face. "There is no doubt what has happened is...bad. However, Kyndra, it can be righted."

"The female wouldn't let me near the male to determine what killed him." Though each dragon order had a leader, Julieth knew the happenings of all the dragons without having to be told by her priestesses.

Julieth sighed. "I know. I saw it."

Kyndra had seen firsthand what Julieth's visions could do.

It amazed Kyndra that Julieth could learn minute details, as if she had experienced what she saw herself.

"I'm sure the female would have struck me had I gotten closer."

"There's no doubt she would have," Julieth agreed and pulled Kyndra with her as they walked to a room behind the throne. She waved for the handmaidens to stay behind then shut the door to face Kyndra. "I can feel the fury moving through all the dragons. There is only one thing that could provoke that kind of anger."

Kyndra's heart plummeted to her feet as the realization hit her. "An egg was stolen."

Julieth nodded. "We cannot know for certain. The Blues mate for life, as you know. The female is mourning the loss of her mate, and her anger is palpable. She distrusts us now."

"They know me. I've never given them reason to do anything but trust us."

"Aye, yet were there not two Fae dead next to her mate?"

Kyndra nodded.

"I've already alerted King Theron. He wishes to speak to you."

"Me?" Kyndra was taken aback. Only the high priestess was called to the palace. "Why me?"

Julieth's face was grave. "Unease ripples through our realm. For months the dragons have watched, waiting to see the next time the dark magic would surface. Whoever is wielding it is very powerful. Not even the dragons can determine who it is."

Kyndra fisted her hands and took a deep breath. "We've all heard of the murders, but it isn't natural for the Fae to turn evil. The magic that pours through our realm—us—is pure."

"There is always a balance of good and evil. You cannot have one without the other. Most Fae who feel the pull of the dark side will leave our realm, for they know to be discovered is to be locked away, or even death."

"Exactly. The few who have dared to fall to the dark have

been discovered. We all know how seductive black magic is."

Julieth shook her head and sliced her hand through the air. "You've read of its seduction, Kyndra. That is vastly different than tasting your first rush from using the black magic. For most, the threat of never seeing our realm again will keep a Fae from trying the black magic. But for others…"

She didn't finish. She didn't need to.

"Why aren't you going to the palace?" Kyndra asked. "King Theron has never called for me before."

Julieth took Kyndra's hands in her own. "No one knows the Blues as you do. You are next in line to take my place. Everyone knows this."

"You have many more years left."

Julieth smiled sadly. "I'm tired, Kyndra. So very tired. Most of my magic is given to keep the black magic that had been used from mixing with the dragon's. It's exhausting and has drained me. The Order needs a warrior. You are our finest."

"I've failed once today. I don't want to fail again."

"Then don't. Trust yourself and your instincts. You've risen through the ranks to lead the Blue Order. Show me the warrior who took the lead, show me the leader I know you are."

Kyndra sighed and turned away from her high priestess. What Julieth asked was an honor, one she would have taken without a second thought a few hours earlier. But now, after she had failed, she didn't want the future of their realm to rest on her shoulders.

"You can do this, Kyndra. I know it."

She faced Julieth. To walk away now would be cowardly, and Kyndra was anything but a coward. "I will do it."

"You won't be alone."

Kyndra narrowed her eyes. "What do you mean?"

"Too much rests on what has happened. The commander of the Fae army, Aimery, will be joining you."

A shiver of foreboding raced over her skin. She had heard

whispers of Aimery from the young girls who came to the temple to be chosen as priestesses. Aimery's power and charm and magnetism were legendary.

"Aimery?"

"He's the best," Julieth said. "Just as you are."

"So be it."

Chapter Three

Aimery let his gaze move over the city. From his chambers in the palace high above *Caer Rhoemyr*, he could see everything. *Caer Rhoemyr*, the city of kings. A city unlike any other in the universe. Beautiful, of course, but it also held the jewels of the Fae—the king and queen.

Aimery inhaled deeply. Nothing seemed out of ordinary, but he had felt the shift in the magic all the way to his bones. The fact there were no dragons flying only added to his worry. Something had happened, but what? And where?

"Aimery!"

He turned at the small voice and bent down in time to see something flying at him in a blur of silver and white. His arms wrapped around the small body as he lifted Nearra to his chest.

"Nearra," Rufina scolded as she stopped at the doorway to Aimery's chamber out of breath with her gaze narrowed on her daughter. "Aimery, I apologize. My child will learn her manners someday."

Aimery laughed and touched his finger to the end of Nearra's pert little nose. "She's fine, Rufina. She knows I enjoy her company. You shouldn't be chasing after her. You have servants to do that, my queen."

She rolled her eyes and ran her hand over her stomach swollen with the realm's second heir. "A few more months and I'll be chasing after two of them. Maybe then I'll get the servants to help, but I don't know if it will work. Nearra has a talent of winding everyone about her little finger, especially you and Theron."

"A little girl is supposed to have her father wrapped around her finger," Aimery said as he walked to his queen. He scooted a chair to her. "Now sit before Theron has my head."

Rufina sank into the chair with a sigh. "We were looking for Theron. Do you know where he is?"

Aimery saw the concern in her blue depths. She had also felt the shift of magic. "I don't know."

"Aimery?" Nearra said as she tapped his cheek. "I came to tell you something."

"What is that, little one?"

She smiled, her many flaxen braids making her look more of a mischievous pixie than a princess to the Fae realm. "I've decided I shall marry you."

"Is that right?" He glanced at Rufina to see her eyes wide in shock.

"Aye," Nearra said. "We get along good, and you know to give me what I want."

Aimery chucked and kissed her forehead. "By the time you're old enough to consider marriage, you won't be thinking of me."

"You're wrong. Trust me."

Aimery was ever surprised by the little minx. He adored her as if she were his own daughter. The longing he had every time he held her only grew. He had thought to have his own children by now, but he had given up ever finding a woman who stirred his heart as well as his blood. "You know I do trust you."

She nodded and grabbed his face with her chubby fingers to kiss his cheek. "You may put me down now. I've more to do."

Aimery set her down, and she raced from his chamber. He

then held out a hand and helped Rufina to her feet. Rufina held a grace that went unmatched by any Fae in the realm. She held the typical long, straight flaxen hair with swirling blue eyes and a lithe figure, but as queen Rufina held something no one else did—Theron's heart. Though Rufina was more of a sister and Theron a brother to him, Aimery couldn't stop the envy of the love they shared.

"That child," Rufina said with a shake of her head as she watched her daughter run down the corridor. "She certainly keeps the palace on its toes."

"She's adorable, and she knows it."

"She is, isn't she? " Her smile vanished, and she faced Aimery. "Something has happened."

"I know. I was about to look for Theron."

"Hurry, Aimery. I fear the worst."

They parted ways at his door. Aimery turned left. He figured he would find Theron in the throne room. Why Theron hadn't called to him already left him nervous. Whatever had happened must be bad. Very bad.

"Aimery."

Finally, Theron's call. Aimery lengthened his strides and hurried to the throne room, the white and bright blue squares of the floor blurring in his haste. The double doors to the throne room opened as he approached.

"Aimery," Theron called and greeted him in the middle of the massive circular room.

"I felt it."

Theron sighed. "Every Fae felt it. Some might not know what it is, but most will."

"How bad is it?"

"Terrible, old friend. Terrible indeed." He ran a down his face and let his weariness show. "A Blue has been killed."

Aimery blew out a breath and shook his head in disbelief. The Blues were their greatest dragons. They weren't the largest, but they had the strongest magic. The realm couldn't sustain another dragon death. "How?"

Theron shrugged his shoulders, his white and blue robes moving with him. "I don't know."

"And the maiden priestesses of the Dragon Order? Have they not determined what killed the Blue?"

"Nay."

Which meant it was far worse than terrible, it was disastrous. "What do you need me to do?"

"It's going to be dangerous."

Aimery grinned. "I live for danger."

Theron returned the smile. "I'm a fool for sending the best warrior we have, but I'd be a fool not to."

"Just tell me what is going on?"

"We don't know what happened to the Blue because the priestess has been unable to get close to the dead dragon to discover what killed him."

Aimery crossed his arms over his chest. He knew enough about the Dragon Order to know each dragon had a sub-order and a leader. Because he was the commander of the Fae army and Theron's right hand man, he knew the names of the leaders.

"Kyndra is the leader of the Blue Order. Has she not tried?"

"She was the first," Theron murmured. "If they won't allow her, they won't allow anyone."

"Not even Julieth?"

"Julieth is...weakening. Her magic has been used against the black magic that seems to have invaded our realm."

Aimery ground his teeth together. "This is related to the string of murders, Theron. I'm sure of it."

"As am I, which is why I've called for you."

"I'll do what must be done."

"I have no doubt."

It was the uncertainty in Theron's swirling blue gaze that made Aimery narrow his eyes. "What aren't you telling me?"

Theron glanced toward an open set of doors that led to the balcony. Aimery followed his gaze and found a cloaked figure with her back to him. The breeze lifted the cloak showing long, lean legs encased in black boots that stopped at her knee. He got a glimpse of pale blue skirts that ended mid thigh.

The dress of a warrior maiden—a maiden of the Dragon Order.

He knew without being told this woman was Kyndra. He'd heard rumors of her infamous beauty, how men had begged for her hand, but she had chosen the virgin robes of a priestess instead.

"Together the two of you will be unstoppable," Theron said. "Together, the two of you can right what went wrong."

At that moment Kyndra turned from the railing and let the hood of her cloak fall back.

Chapter Four

Aimery's breath locked in his lungs as he stared at the wealth of dark hair that fell over her shoulder to her waist. It was uncommon for a Fae to have any color but flaxen, yet before him stood the rarest of the rare.

It wasn't just her brunette locks either. As a general rule all Fae were sensual, beautiful creatures, but beautiful didn't begin to describe Kyndra. She was elegant, magnificent…visually stunning.

She had high cheekbones and dark brows that arched over wide, expressive eyes. Her full lips held a hint of a smile, as if she knew her affect on men. Wisps of hair curled about her face and slender neck. Her gown molded to her full breasts and narrow waist. Aimery longed to run his hands up her toned legs, kissing every inch of her skin.

Her swirling blue eyes held his as if she were sizing him up. But he didn't care. He couldn't tear his eyes from her. A warrior. A priestess. And a woman every Fae in the realm longed to possess.

What in all that was magical had Theron been thinking to put him in this position?

Theron cleared his throat, and Aimery forced his gaze

away.

"Aimery," he said, "this is Kyndra, leader of the Blue Order and next in line for high priestess of the Dragon Order."

Aimery glanced at Kyndra to find she had moved closer to him, her gaze raking over him as his had done to her just moments earlier. Did she like what she saw? As soon as the thought went through his head he knew it was useless. She was a maiden, her life vowed to the dragons and her order. No man could touch her.

"Kyndra," Theron continued. "This is Aimery, commander of the Fae armies and Duke of Eldwinds."

"A duke?" she repeated, her voice smooth, soft. Mesmerizing.

Aimery clenched his teeth. Theron knew he didn't want his title bandied about, because it was just a title and meant nothing. "The title has been in my family for generations."

Her brows rose before her gaze shifted to Theron. "I would like to state now that I would prefer Julieth be here in my place."

"I know," Theron said. "Julieth told me as much, but she doesn't have the strength. As next in line for her position, this will give you ample opportunity to test your skills."

"You make it sound like a holiday, sire, when in fact our realm is at stake."

Theron glanced at Aimery. "You'll have the finest warrior of our people at your side. I wouldn't dare think to send you on a mission you couldn't handle. Julieth praised your skill. Was she wrong to recommend you?"

Kyndra's chin rose. "Nay. I won't let our people down."

"Where are we going?" Aimery asked.

Kyndra felt Theron's eyes on her. She swallowed and forced herself to meet Aimery's gaze. "I don't know."

His brow furrowed. "You haven't been to the Blue yet? You haven't looked?"

"Of course I have," she said through clenched teeth. Her ire rose at the condescending tone the commander used. "It is my duty to go to them as soon as something happens."

"Then what did you see?"

Kyndra took in a calming breath and lowered her gaze to the blue and white tiles. "The female wouldn't let me near the male. I've never seen a dragon so angry before. Without learning what caused the Blue's death, we might never know who to find or where they went."

"The Blues know you. You need to try again. Maybe the female has calmed down by now."

She lifted her gaze to Aimery. He was more handsome than she had anticipated. The rumors of his sexuality and striking good looks were nothing compared to the gorgeous specimen before her.

His flaxen hair hung down his back thick and straight. Several rows of braids were woven near his temples in intricate designs, and the light blue tunic stitched with silver thread showed the breadth and width of his muscular shoulders. She tried not to look into his eyes of swirling blue, but too easily his caught and held her. With his square jaw, wide mouth, and expressive eyes, she was surprised he hadn't already found a wife.

"Shall we return to dragons then?" he asked.

There was no other choice really. They had to know what happened. "Aye. Be warned, the female is out for blood."

"We'll be ready."

Since he wore no weapons, she wasn't so sure of that. It was a good thing she had brought her sword. "Follow me."

Kyndra transported to the mountains, a safe distance away so they could see the dragons without being attacked. In a blink, Aimery and Theron stood on either side of her.

"By the gods," Theron murmured.

Just looking at the dead Blue made Kyndra's heart ache. The female stood near her mate, her roars of grief echoing through the mountains. All around them dragons had begun to come, watching the female. They flew across the sky while others landed and watched.

"Do you feel her pain?" Aimery asked.

Kyndra nodded. "The depth of her anguish is staggering."

"Come, Kyndra. We must learn what happened."

She was prepared to go alone, not with Aimery and the king with her. "I don't think it wise that you follow me."

Theron smiled. "We'll be fine. Lead on, priestess."

Kyndra walked toward the dragon, her nerves tensing when the female turned her dark eyes on her. There was hatred there, something Kyndra had never seen in a dragon's eyes before. It gave her pause and told her the magnitude of the female's anger.

"Be careful," she said over her shoulder. "The female's rage grows."

By the time they reached the dragon, Kyndra was having serious doubts that any of them would come away unscathed. The female had spread her wings and began to growl. With every step Kyndra took toward the male, the female readied to strike.

"Let me," Aimery said.

Kyndra jerked her gaze to him. "You don't have dealings with the dragons. If she doesn't allow me near her mate, what makes you think you can get to him?"

Aimery shrugged his shoulders. "A hunch."

Kyndra opened her mouth to argue when Theron placed a hand on her arm. "Give him a chance. He just might surprise you."

She doubted it, but what choice did she have when the king commanded her? She watched as Aimery moved to the male. He stopped and looked at each of the dead Fae before he turned to them and shook his head.

"He doesn't recognize them," Theron said. "I was hoping he would know who they were."

Kyndra fisted her hands when the female turned her head to Aimery. She wasn't happy about being paired with Aimery, but she didn't want to see the commander die.

"We're here to help," he told the dragon. "Let me see who

dared to kill your mate so that we may bring them to you for justice."

The female stared at him for the longest time before she returned to her roars of grief. Kyndra was stunned. Why was the Blue allowing Aimery near her mate and not her? Most of her life had been dedicated to the Blues, so it was more than galling to have Aimery earn the dragon's trust so easily.

Aimery glanced at Kyndra to see her mouth pinched in anger. It wasn't how he wanted to begin their partnership, but it was a chance he'd had to take. He knelt by the dead male and sighed. The Blues' magic made up for their size. It was the reason the Fae had chosen to take blue as their color. Even being one of the smaller dragons, its size was still staggering.

He laid his hand on the male's shoulder. His breath was sucked from his lungs as he saw through the dragon's eyes. Three men, two who

had dared to enter the lair and take their most prized possession—an egg.

The male had managed to kill them. Then the dragon had looked at the third man. Aimery bellowed as he saw his friend, Isran, with the egg at his feet. Aimery didn't think his betrayal could cut any deeper until he saw Isran call the black magic that had killed the male.

Aimery released the male and lowered his head into his hands. Fury ripped through him, and the need for vengeance turned his blood to ice. He lifted his gaze to the female. "By my very life I vow to return to you the Fae who killed your mate, and I will do everything in my power to bring your egg back to you."

The female lay down next to her mate and closed her eyes. Aimery rose on shaky legs and without a word returned to the palace. He needed to prepare. Isran had left their realm, and with a dragon's egg there were only a few places he would dare to go.

Aimery stripped off his clothes and reached for his battle gear. He had just fastened his breeches when he felt the air stir around him.

"What happened?" Theron asked.

He paused for a moment before he sat and pulled on his boots.

"Aimery."

With a curse he faced his king to see Kyndra standing behind Theron. "We travel outside our realm. You best prepare."

"Aimery," Theron bellowed. "Tell me what you saw!"

Aimery closed his eyes and tried to rein in his rioting emotions. "They didn't just kill the male. They took an egg."

Kyndra gasped and grasped the doorway to help steady her.

A tick jumped in Theron's jaw. "Who would dare such a thing?"

"Isran," Aimery ground out.

"He wouldn't," Theron said.

Aimery snorted. "I saw him. I saw him take the egg, and I saw him use black magic."

For long moments no one said anything. Aimery ran a hand down his face, eager to begin looking for the bastard who had fooled him so.

"The betrayal cuts deep," Theron said. "For all of us, but for you most of all because you considered him a brother. At least now we know who has been murdering the other Fae."

Aimery jerked on his tunic and reached for his sword. "I'm going to find him no matter how long it takes."

Theron stepped into his chamber and placed a hand on his shoulder. "You've led my army meticulously for years, old friend. Don't let your emotions rule you now. Think."

"I am thinking. Isran is going to pay for what he's done."

"I've no doubt." Theron sighed and dropped his arm to pace the chamber. "If Isran has taken the egg, it's because he's using it to gain coin."

Kyndra moved into the chamber and leaned against the open door. "There aren't many who would dare to anger us by accepting a dragon's egg or a traitor."

21

Aimery reached for his dagger, a massive curved blade that would sever a head from a body. He strapped it on his waist before slinging the strap to his scabbard over his head so that his sword rested on his back.

"I've an idea where to start," he said. "Thav."

Kyndra visibly shuddered while Theron paled. "Aimery, no Fae has come back from that realm. It is a pit for thieves and mercenaries and cheats. Even when Lugus has gone as emissary it's always a gamble if he'll be able to return."

"Which means it is the perfect place for Isran to take the egg. Someone will be willing to pay what Isran wants for the egg."

"But why take the egg at all?" Kyndra asked. "Why kill the male?"

"He killed the male because he could. He knew we would discover it was him. He wants me to come looking for him."

Theron nodded. "I agree. I think he took the egg not because of coin."

Kyndra's blood turned to ice when Aimery laughed, the sound hollow and devoid of mirth. Ever since the commander had touched the blue dragon he hadn't been able to hold back his anger, or maybe he didn't want to. She didn't know who Isran was but, whoever he was, the treachery to Aimery was severe.

She glanced at his chest, disappointed that he had put on the tunic, but the glimpse she had seen of sculpted muscles had been well worth it.

As he gathered his weapons for battle, she knew their journey would be treacherous, most likely claiming both their lives.

"You're right," Aimery said. "Isran isn't after coin. He's after power. The black magic he's been using is demanding more. He will continue until he has the power to invade us."

"That won't ever happen." Theron crossed his arms over his chest. "I'm sealing all doors in and out of our realm."

Aimery shook his head. "It won't stop Isran, not for long

anyway. If he gets the power he needs, he'll be able to move through time and space much like Lugus does."

Kyndra listened with interest. Everyone knew of Lugus. As brother to Theron and rightful heir to the throne, he had been wrongly accused and thrown into the Realm of Shadows to die. Only he hadn't died. He had managed to live through it, growing stronger until his powers were great enough to get out of the realm and try to take over the Fae as well as Earth. He nearly succeeded, but he gave his immortality to save their realm, thereby giving him a second chance at life.

Though Lugus had been forbidden to ever return to the Realm of the Fae, he had done so to find Theron who had been tricked into the Realm of Shadows. That feat, as well as the love of a Fae, had returned his immortality. To the surprise of all, he hadn't claimed the throne as was his right.

"Lugus can travel wherever he chooses?" she asked.

Theron nodded. "I've already called him here. He'll help us."

"You shouldn't have," Aimery said. "Ahryn is ready to give birth to their first child. He needs to be here for that."

"I'll let him decide." Theron turned on his heel and walked from the chamber.

Kyndra glanced from the king to Aimery. "Where is he going?"

"To the throne room to await Lugus."

She licked her lips and pushed from the door. "Thank you for getting the information we needed."

"I'm surprised you aren't angry with me because of it."

"Oh, I am perturbed about it."

A faint smile pulled at his lips. "You still have the Blue's trust, Kyndra. Never doubt that. Anger and grief can make anything lose focus."

He motioned for her to follow Theron. Aimery fell into step beside her, and she found that she didn't mind him being near. She had seen his appreciative glance over her body, but he hadn't attempted to gain her interest. Not that he needed to do anything. No one could be in a room and not notice Aimery. He exuded sexuality greater than any Fae she had ever encountered. Add that to his magnetism and it was near impossible to stay away from him.

Which was going to make being alone with him her greatest test.

Chapter Five

Kyndra stopped beside Aimery in the throne room to see Theron and Lugus in a conversation. "Do you know Lugus?"

"Aye. The three of us grew up together," Aimery answered. "He's a good man who had a terrible wrong done to him."

"Everything worked out in the end, didn't it?"

"It did. Yet for all that happened, I know Lugus will always carry the weight upon his shoulders. He would have made a good king."

His answer intrigued her. "Would you have honored him as your king had he wanted the throne?"

Aimery's gaze swung to her. "It's his by right of birth. Even if he wanted to claim it now, he has every right, and Theron knows it."

"Will Lugus ever claim it?"

"I doubt it. He doesn't feel as though he's worthy of the crown. He also has a good life with Ahryn, his wife. He's found happiness and peace. What more could a man want?"

"What indeed," she murmured.

Aimery faced her and crossed his arms over his chest. "What about you, priestess? What do you want?"

"What I have now. Being a priestess to the Dragon Order is

all I've ever wanted."

"How would you know? How would any of the virgins who make their way to the temple know? You've not known the caress of a man. How could you deny what comes naturally to us?"

"We all have our calling, Commander. For me it was to pledge myself to the Order and the dragons. It is a worthy cause, one I'm extremely proud of. Just as, I'm sure, you are proud to lead the army."

"Nicely done."

She smiled. "Is what Theron said of Thav true?"

"I'm not going to lie to you, Kyndra. It's very dangerous. I wouldn't take you with me, but Theron has commanded it."

"A priestess I might be, but I can also hold my own with a sword."

"I'd like to say we won't find out, but we probably will."

Excitement coursed through Kyndra. This was her time to prove she was the next high priestess. This was her time to right the wrong done to the Blues. And she wouldn't fail.

"Aimery, Kyndra," Theron called.

They walked to the king and his brother. Lugus' hair was darker than Aimery's, and he was several inches taller than Theron. Also, his build was more like Aimery's instead of the lithe body of the king.

"Kyndra of the Blue Order," Lugus said as he bowed his head to her. "Theron has told me he sends you with Aimery after Isran and the egg."

"He does, your highness."

Lugus held up a hand. "None of that. I'm simply Lugus."

She smiled, liking him instantly. It was then she noticed the many tattoos on his hands, forearms, and neck.

"Aye," Lugus said.

She blinked. "I'm sorry?"

"You wondered if the tattoos are on other parts of my body. They are. My chest and arms are covered in them."

Theron shook his head with a smile. "Those tattoos are

what will get us to Thav."

"I don't understand," Kyndra said. "How can a tattoo help?"

Lugus glanced at the ground. "At one point I had a vast amount of power. With these tattoos I'm able to command magic to transport me wherever I need to go. Each tattoo is a realm."

"Amazing."

He shrugged and faced Aimery. "Hello, old friend."

They clasped forearms before they hugged. "You should come to the palace more often," Aimery said.

"And you should come to the house more often. Ahryn is beginning to think you don't like her cooking."

Theron laughed. "Don't let him lie to you, Aimery. Ahryn doesn't cook. They might live in the mountains, but they have nearly as many servants as I do."

"Now who's lying," Lugus said.

Kyndra watched the exchange with a smile. For all his faults, Lugus had righted a great wrong. Surely she could do the same.

"I'll be sure to visit once this is all over," Aimery promised.

The smile on Lugus' face dropped. "I'll tell you all right now, I don't advise going to Thav. I've visited it four times, and it was four times too many. It is an unholy place, a place drenched in black magic."

Kyndra waited for the others to ask why and, when they didn't, she did. "Why?"

"The ruler of Thav, a beastly man named Eldar, doesn't like anyone to have more magic than he does. He limits the use of black magic, and our magic…he cuts off all together."

Aimery let out a string of curses.

"I can't let them go someplace they can't use magic," Theron said.

Kyndra was shaken to her core at the news. "We have to go. Our realm is at stake."

Lugus narrowed his gaze on her. "Have you ever been

without magic, priestess?"

"You know I haven't."

"Well, I have. Five years that felt more like five millennia. My wife went several months without the use of her magic. For a Fae who has known nothing but magic, it will be impossible for you to live with."

"I have no other choice. I have to get the egg back." She looked at the three men. "There was always a measure of danger in this mission; knowing that it's taking us to a realm we'd rather not go changes nothing. We have to go."

Aimery's blood heated just watching Kyndra. With one look from her, he would have done anything she asked. "She's right, Theron. We have to go. Lugus doesn't. Open the doorway long enough for us to get through before you close it again."

"How will you return?" Theron asked. "Especially if you cannot use magic."

"We'll have to plan on enticing Eldar. All leaders have a weakness, and Thav is no different."

"Nay," Theron said. "I cannot risk it."

"You cannot risk them not going after Isran. You know as well as I they have to go." Lugus faced Aimery. "However, I will be going with you."

"Nay. You need to be here for the birth of your child."

"I agree. Which means we need to come up with a plan that will ensure I'm here."

Aimery sighed and paced the round chamber.

"What does a man such as Eldar want?" Kyndra asked.

Aimery answered without thought. "Power. He hungers for power."

"Much like Isran does."

"Correct," Lugus said.

Kyndra shrugged. "Then why is Isran going to the very man who will limit his use of black magic."

Aimery dropped his head back as realization ran through him.

"What is it?" Theron asked.

Aimery met his king's gaze. "Isran isn't going to Thav to seek Eldar's help. He's going to Thav to usurp the throne. With the dragon's egg at his side, he will be able to prove that he's more powerful than Eldar."

"And with Eldar's death, Isran will claim his power," Lugus finished.

"Shite." Theron moved to his throne and sank onto the seat. "Are you sure?"

Aimery nodded. "I'd stake my life on it."

"You might very well have to," Lugus said.

Aimery looked to Kyndra to find her mouth pinched and her brow furrowed. Her parlor was paling with each moment.

"Isran has the egg, which means he plans to use it. For leverage to get followers?" Theron asked.

"That's a possibility." Aimery took a step toward Kyndra as her chest began to rise and fall rapidly.

Lugus shrugged. "Or he'll crack open the egg and bathe in the undeveloped dragon embryo which will enable him to rule the Blues."

Aimery caught Kyndra as she swayed. Her fingers clutched at his arm, her eyes wide with fear. "How do you know that?"

Aimery threw Lugus a disgusted look as Kyndra's nails sunk into his flesh.

"The dragons are an important part of our lives," Lugus said. "It is imperative that the king and his advisors know all there is to know of the dragons."

Kyndra's gaze met Aimery's.

Theron nodded. "The Order does know everything involving the dragons, except when it comes to black magic."

"We aren't taught anything with black magic," Kyndra said.

"It's one of the reasons we're so careful to capture any Fae who delves into the black arts."

"We can't let him succeed."

"No, we can't," Aimery said.

At his words, she took in a shaky breath and released his arm. "I've failed my order once already. I refuse to do it twice."

"Then you're going to need my help," Lugus said. "Let's get a plan together. We've wasted enough time already, and I want to return to my wife."

Aimery set Kyndra on her feet. It was only after he released her that he realized how much he enjoyed holding her soft body. His balls tightened just thinking of touching her again.

But you can't have her.

That was what ate at him the most. She wasn't for him. She had chosen the dragons over the pleasures of the flesh. There was nothing he could do or say to dissuade her from her vows, and he didn't want to. He respected her choice, but it was going to be damn hard remembering that he couldn't touch her.

"We need to get in to see Eldar," he said. "If we can convince him why we're there, we might be able to get him on our side."

"And possibly the use of our magic?" Kyndra asked.

Aimery shrugged. "It's a possibility, but I wouldn't count on it."

"That's a good idea," Theron said. "Do you think you can get in to see Eldar before Isran?"

"Knowing Isran, he went to Thav as soon as he had the egg. Once on Thav, he set about hatching his plan. He likes to work alone, but he will gain help if needed. He showed that at the dragon's lair."

Lugus smiled then. "I know how to get us in to see Eldar."

"How?"

"Am I not an emissary to Theron? Is it not a custom of all realms to allow emissaries entrance before others?"

Aimery threw back his head and laughed. "Lugus, you're brilliant."

Theron clapped his brother on the back. "I'll write up a missive for you to take to Eldar."

30

Chapter Six

Kyndra tried to shake off the warmth of Aimery's hold. No man had touched her since she left her home and said farewell to her father. Not even King Theron dared to touch her.

But Aimery hadn't thought twice about it.

It made her wonder if going alone with him to Thav was such a good idea. Yet, she had no choice. Regardless of how his touch made her blood heat and her heart accelerate. She had taken vows. Those vows meant everything to her, the dragons meant everything to her. There was nothing that would make her turn her back on the Order or the dragons.

She turned to find Lugus leaning over Theron who sat behind a massive desk, ornately decorated with the knot work of the Fae. She watched the brothers for a moment, still unable to believe Lugus would allow Theron to keep the throne when it was rightfully his.

The smell of orangewood filled her senses. She inhaled the scent, immediately recognizing it was Aimery a moment before he stepped into her line of vision. Her gaze was drawn to him. Stories of his feats had circulated the realm for millennia. He was feared among the Fae, as well as trusted. Theron had indeed chosen the right warrior to send after Isran.

Aimery's swirling blue gaze met hers. He had retrieved more weapons and a jerkin of deep blue. His flaxen hair still had the small plaits at his temples, but they had been pulled back, along with the rest of his hair, to a queue at the base of his neck.

He hid his emotions well, but Kyndra had seen the fury and anguish by Isran's betrayal. In a way she felt sorry for Isran, because once Aimery found him, and she had no doubt the commander would find him, the retribution would be terrible.

Kyndra wanted her chance at Isran herself. There was nothing either she or Aimery could do that could match what the dragons would do to him, but the need to punish him, to inflict harm upon a Fae who would dare to harm a dragon was too much to ignore.

She shifted the cloak over her shoulders. Aimery's gaze lowered to the dragon band about her left arm. It let all know that she wasn't just a priestess, but a warrior for the dragons. It had been one of her most glorious days when she had earned the right to wear the dragon.

"Are you ready?"

Kyndra jerked her gaze to the king. Theron was staring at her. He rose and leaned his hands on the desk, his gaze intense.

She gave a small nod. "I'm ready."

"Kyndra, I know I chose you to go with Aimery," Theron said. "However, that was before I knew who had taken the egg and where he had gone."

Kyndra opened her mouth to argue with Theron when Aimery stepped forward. "We're ready."

The king and Lugus swung their gazes to Aimery. Theron ran a hand down his face and straightened. "I want all three of you to return. The thought of losing any one of you…"

"We'll return." Lugus walked around the desk to stand on her left, putting her between him and Aimery.

A fission of fear raced along her spine, but she refused to let any of them see it. She gripped the hilt of her sword to give her strength. It wasn't that she feared facing Isran or even going into a realm such as Thav. What she feared most was not be able to call upon her magic.

Magic had been a part of every Fae's training from the moment of his birth. It was no wonder so many went insane when not able to use it. Her gaze fell on Lugus. He had survived for five years without it. Five years to a Fae were gone in a blink but, to a Fae who had been mortal on Earth, it must have felt like eternity.

Lugus had survived. She would survive. All she had to do was remember the look in the blue dragon's eyes as she gazed at her dead mate to give her the courage and strength Kyndra needed to finish her mission.

Theron walked around his desk to stand in front of them. "Let the magic of the realm and the well wishes of every Fae follow you on your quest."

"We're going to need it," Lugus said. He pushed the sleeve on his left arm up to reveal the tattoos. "Ready?"

She nodded, her gaze on the tattoos.

"We've wasted enough time," Aimery said.

Lugus' fingers hovered over a tattoo near his elbow. It was the size of a small coin and looked like an eye with some strange writing around it. "Keep watch on Ahryn for me."

"You have my word," Theron said.

And with that, Lugus placed his finger on the eye.

Kyndra blinked, the darkness around her causing fear to well up inside her.

"Kyndra?"

She sighed. Aimery was with her. "I'm here. Why can't I see?"

Lugus let out a long sigh. "Its Eldar's spell. Our magic is gone."

"You weren't jesting that it would be gone as soon as we entered the realm. " Kyndra flexed her shoulders. She didn't like not being able to see. She hadn't realized until then that her sight had been enhanced by magic. She began to wonder just what else was enhanced by magic, and she had a suspicion it was much more than she realized.

"Are you all right?"

Aimery's breath fanned her skin as he whispered in her ear. The heat from his body surrounded her, and she knew all she had to do was lean back and she'd find him against her. It should irritate her, but it didn't. She was glad he was there, because she was going to be tested. And she feared how she would react.

"We're in some kind of structure," Lugus said. He grunted as he moved forward and collided with something. "Stay here until I find the door."

To her amazement, he navigated the room without running into anything else. "How are you doing that?"

"I remembered what it's like not to be able to see," Lugus answered. "It didn't take long for my eyes to become adjusted to the darkness. Yours will as well."

Aimery grunted. "I don't plan to be here that long."

"Let's hope you're right." No sooner had Lugus spoke than moonlight poured into the room.

Kyndra had the urge to shout for joy. With Aimery at her back she walked to Lugus and out of the building. "Now what?"

Aimery shut the door and pulled her into the shadows. His gazed raked over their surroundings. "Where are we, Lugus?"

"The capital city. Eldar's castle is there," he said and pointed high above them.

Kyndra followed Lugus' finger, craning her neck to look at the top of the mountain and the fortress that rested at the top. "Of course."

Lugus chuckled then drew in a quick breath, his hand to his head.

"Lugus?" Aimery stepped to him, grabbing his friend by the shoulders. "What is it?"

"Ahryn," he answered in a strangled whisper.

Kyndra looked from Lugus to Aimery. "What is going on? How can Lugus know about his wife if our magic is stopped?"

Aimery held Lugus steady as he swayed on his feet. Whatever Ahryn was telling him wasn't good. "Ahryn is able to communicate with Lugus through her mind, regardless of where he is."

"By all that's magic," Kyndra murmured.

Lugus fell to his knees, his face ashen and his mouth twisted in pain. "It's the babe. She's in labor, Aimery, and she's dying."

"Go to her." Aimery wouldn't let anything stop him from being with his wife in such a time. Ahryn needed Lugus much more than they did.

Lugus' eyes opened to stare at him. "I cannot leave you. You need me."

"And she needs you more. Go to your wife."

"You're going to need this."

Aimery took the scroll Theron had written and tucked it in his jerkin. "Don't worry about us. We'll be fine."

"I'm sorry," Lugus whispered before he touched another tattoo, this one on his right hand, and vanished before their eyes.

Aimery sighed and sat back on his heels. He turned to Kyndra to find her eyes wide, staring at the spot where Lugus had just been kneeling. Aimery forced away the terror that clawed at him and stood. He held out his hand to Kyndra and pulled her to her feet. She looked up at him with trusting eyes, and he knew then he would do whatever it took to ensure she made it back to their realm.

"Lugus having to leave is a minor setback. We've got the missive from Theron, which should enable us to see Eldar."

Kyndra licked her lips, drawing Aimery's gaze to them. "You seem so confident of everything."

He was anything but, but he wasn't going to let her know that. "We'll be fine. Trust me."

"I do."

He hadn't expected her to answer but, now that she had, he was glad of it. He turned his attention to Eldar's castle. The climb would be steep and no doubt overrun with creatures and traps for anyone who didn't know the way.

"What if Isran has already gained control?"

Aimery glanced at her over his shoulder. "There hasn't been enough time."

"How much time does he need to take over a realm?"

"Eldar is extremely powerful. Isran only ever dabbled in black magic, which makes Eldar almost invincible."

"Almost?"

Aimery smiled. "Why is it, do you think, that he takes away other's magic? Our magic is some of the strongest in the universe, Kyndra. We've defeated black magic before, and we will do so again."

"Aye, but has any of them ever had a dragon's egg?"

"That changes nothing."

"He knows how much that egg means to us."

"Exactly," Aimery said and faced her. "Isran knows we'll be hunting him. If we're lucky, he'll think he has a few more days before we come here, when in fact we're already here and will be pleading our case to Eldar."

"It galls me that we have to plead anything to Eldar. He should turn Isran over to us to be dealt with."

Aimery smiled at her indignation. "That is the Fae way. We aren't in our realm anymore. Remember that. They do things much differently here. Thav is a realm where evil gathers to hide from the rest."

"And we're without our magic. We're at Eldar's mercy, Aimery. Anything can happen to us between now and gaining an audience with him."

"Which is why we need to keep moving." He took her arm and guided her down an alley.

She kept in step with him, her eyes seeking into the darkness just as he was. "How large is this city?"

"Too bloody large."

Aimery caught a glimpse of something out of the corner of his eye. He pulled his dagger free and turned to his left to find a creature with half his face burned off coming at him. He ducked as a meaty fist came at his face. As he straightened, he plunged the dagger into the belly of the beast. The creature gave a grunt of pain. Aimery stepped back and withdrew his weapon.

The beast stared at him with his one good eye. He reached for Aimery with one of his long arms, which Aimery easily avoided. Black goo oozed from the wound Aimery had inflicted. The creature pitched forward before he crumpled to the ground.

"What is that?" Kyndra asked as she stood beside him.

Aimery shrugged. "I've never seen the like before. Let's move on."

They hurried through the streets, stopping every now and again when something moved in the shadows. Aimery didn't like the city. It held too many vantage points for others and none for him and Kyndra. Once on the mountain, he would feel safer. Once in the castle and speaking to Eldar, then he would feel as though they stood a chance.

Aimery halted and pushed Kyndra against a building, his arm across her front. Her hand came up and held on to him. He felt the slight tremble in her fingers, and he hated that he couldn't give her a measure of safety.

"What is it?" she whispered.

He shrugged, unable to determine what had made him stop. He detected nothing but, in a place such as Thav, nothing could be your death.

"Stay against the buildings."

Aimery kept his hand on Kyndra as they moved slowly through the shadows. There was movement up ahead, but of what he didn't know. It wasn't until he reached the three-story structure and heard the music that he realized why there was so much activity.

"It's a pub," he murmured.

No sooner had he said the words than a woman walked out of the door nude, her small breasts swaying as she walked. As soon as she stopped, a man stepped out of the shadows and cupped her breast, giving her nipple a pinch.

Her head tilted back, and a sigh reached them when the man began to suckle her nipple. Aimery wondered if Kyndra had ever seen a man and woman together to realize what they were doing. The subtle shift of her feet told him she was uncomfortable.

The woman's head lifted and looked right at Aimery. "Who's there?" she demanded.

"Bloody Hell," Aimery growled and jerked Kyndra to him. There wasn't time for words, not if he wanted to get them out alive.

He turned so that he flattened her against the building and put his back to the woman. Kyndra's soft body met his, and Aimery barely held back a moan as desire shot through him. Her lips parted in question and, before she could speak, he covered her mouth with his.

Chapter Seven

Kyndra forgot to breathe as Aimery's lips moved over hers. The shock of it left her stiff, but the feel of his tongue against her lips made her blood heat. His arms molded her body to his, pushing her against the building. She never knew the hard length of a man could feel so…exhilarating.

Her hands gripped his arms, the muscles beneath her fingers straining. His head titled as his tongue swept between her lips to touch hers. Of their own accord, her arms wrapped around his neck. His body moved against hers, sending ripples of pleasure bursting through her to center between her legs in a deep throb.

Just as suddenly as he had kissed her, he lifted his head.

"I had to think fast," he whispered.

She nodded, unsure of what to say, or if she should say anything. No one had ever kissed her before and, now that Aimery had, she found she enjoyed it entirely too much. She tried to get her breathing under control, but every time she thought of Aimery's mouth her heart accelerated again.

"Kyndra."

She forced her gaze to meet Aimery's. *Pull yourself*

together. It was just a kiss. Just a kiss that had left her rattled, weak. Vulnerable.

His brow furrowed. "I'm not going to apologize for kissing you. I know you took vows, but I will do whatever I must to keep you alive."

Kyndra wanted to touch her lips. They felt swollen, sensitive. Had one kiss done that to her? One, simple kiss?

She glanced around Aimery's shoulder and saw the nude woman pointing at them while talking to two men. "Kiss me."

"What?"

"They're coming this way. Kiss me."

Kyndra knew she must have gone daft. Only a crazy person haven taken her same vows would tempt herself by kissing Aimery. Again.

There was no soft meeting of the lips this time. When Aimery took her mouth, he brought her hard against his body. Her nipples hardened, yearning for something she didn't understand. His hands caressed her back as he deepened the kiss, slanting his mouth over hers again and again.

If Kyndra had thought his first kiss had made her knees weak, this kiss took her breath away. She was drowning in his kiss, and she loved every moment of it. His lips were soft yet firm, and his kiss was unrelenting and fierce. She moved her hands over his wide shoulders, learning the hard feel of him. When she felt his rod, swollen and hard, press against her stomach, a moan escaped her.

He stiffened and ended the kiss. Kyndra hated that she wanted to beg him to kiss her, to make her body come alive as it seemed to do in his hands.

"What are ye doin'?" demanded a voice behind Aimery.

Aimery shifted his head to the side and growled.

A little thrill shot through Kyndra. She knew Aimery was acting for her benefit, keeping her alive, but she couldn't help allowing a part of her to think he did it for her, and her alone.

The man backed away, his arms raised. "All right. No need ta be gettin' riled."

Kyndra fought the urge to bury her head in Aimery's shoulder. Instead, she watched the man drag the nude woman inside the building.

A few moments later, Aimery looked at her. "Is he gone?"

"Yes."

Aimery released her and took a step away. He stared at her, as if he wanted to say something.

Kyndra didn't need his words, nor did she want to explore depth of the desire pumping through her and her attraction to Aimery. They had been in Thav but a few hours, and already she had kissed him twice.

"Let's not tarry here," she said and moved past him.

Thankfully, Aimery fell into step beside her. She wished it were light enough so she could see his face but, then again, the feelings he had brought from her were too fresh for her to hide away. If he looked at her now, he would see the desire and hunger in her gaze, and she couldn't allow that. Not now.

Not ever.

It would take just one word from her, and she knew Aimery would make love to her. She felt it in the way he caressed her, kissed her. She was going to have to be the one to stand against the temptation he offered her.

Not that she blamed him. He had done the only thing he could think of to keep them safe. There was no telling how many men were inside the building drinking and whoring. Aimery wouldn't take the chance if they were outnumbered. It had been a tactical call, and one she agreed with.

Unable to stop herself, she reached up and touched her lips. They felt foreign to her now. She hadn't realized it would feel so...good...to be kissed or that her lips could feel so very much. Lips had meant nothing to her a few moments ago. Now, she would never be able to look at Aimery's mouth again without thinking of their kiss.

They made it safely to the wall of the city. She crouched beside Aimery and looked at the wall before them.

"The gate is being watched," he said. "We'll never get

through it without raising attention. I'd rather Isran not know we're here yet."

"He could already be at the castle."

"Maybe. In which case, it's just another reason to keep our presence a secret until we get to the castle."

She shrugged. "Then we go over the wall."

He glanced at the wall and seemed to consider her suggestion. "I can give you a leg up, but I don't know what's on the other side."

"I'm not without my own skills." She fingered her sword and raised a brow.

Aimery nodded. "All right, but as soon as you get to the other side wait for me."

"Agreed."

She stood and waited for him to lace his fingers together before bracing his hands against his knee. "Ready?"

"Ready."

Kyndra took a few steps back before she ran at him and used his laced hands as a foot hold. As soon as her foot met his hands, he tossed her up. She landed half on top of the wall with a grunt. She pulled herself up and realized the wall was three feet thick.

She leaned over and gave Aimery a wave before she unsheathed her sword and dropped onto the other side. There was no movement, no shout that she had been seen, but Kyndra wasn't taking any chances.

A few moments later Aimery dropped down beside her.

"You got over faster than I expected."

He grinned. "I'm not without my skills."

Kyndra turned away so he wouldn't see her smile. They had gotten out of the city, but they still had to navigate the mountain. And the castle. "The terrain looks flat before we get to the mountain."

"It could be, but we'll have to be careful. Not only is it flat, but there are no trees or anything to hide against. If anyone looks out, they'll be able to see us."

"We'll have to make a run for it and pray no one sees us."

"We need to find some place to rest. I don't want to get on that mountain in the dark."

She sheathed her sword. "I disagree. It's the best time to climb it."

"There are traps laid out all along the mountain. That was one of the reasons Lugus was with us. He was going to show us the way in."

Kyndra sighed and leaned her head against the wall. "You're right then. We need to be able to see where we're going."

"I'll get us to the castle."

She turned her head to Aimery. She had no doubt he would give his life to make sure she found the egg. "I know."

He took her hand and pulled her after him as he darted across the open land, only it wasn't flat as they had thought. The terrain undulated, making their run that much more treacherous.

Kyndra glanced over her shoulder once, but no one at the gates had noticed them. She was just about to tell Aimery when a loud squawk sounded above them. She looked up to find a giant bird. Aimery cursed and lengthened his strides. Kyndra had no choice but to do the same or be dragged behind him.

"Duck," she shouted as the bird dove at them.

Aimery wrapped his arms around her and fell to the ground. They hit the ground and fell over a hill and began to roll. Kyndra wrapped her arms around Aimery and buried her head in his chest.

And then suddenly, there was nothing.

A scream formed in Kyndra's throat, but before she could get it out, they landed with a resounding thud. All the breath was knocked from her body. She tried to breathe, to get air in her lungs, but they refused to work.

"Don't fight it," Aimery said as he sat up.

He lifted her in his arms and tucked them in the shadows

while the bird circled overhead, screaming its rage.

Kyndra was finally able to get air in her lungs. Her body ached, but she was comfortable in Aimery's arms. She should move, she knew that, but she didn't have the will to do it.

"Are you hurt?"

"I don't think so. Where are we?"

She felt his shrug. "It looks like a canyon. I don't know how big it is, but it's a good place for us to rest and hide."

"From a giant bird."

He chuckled. "You've never been out of our realm. You have no idea what's out there waiting to be discovered. There are things you wouldn't believe."

"And you've seen them?"

"I've seen so very much."

"What's it like?" she asked. "Do you like leaving our realm?"

He shifted. "I do like to see other realms, but the call of our realm is always with me. I can never stay away too long. As a priestess, you can't travel can you?"

"No." It had never bothered her before, but now that she had left their realm, the yearning to see other realms had begun to grow.

"That's too bad. I think you would enjoy it."

Unfortunately, so did she.

Chapter Eight

Aimery tore his hungry gaze from Kyndra's sleeping form and watched the sun rise over the mountain. He had spent the remainder of the darkness reliving their kisses over and over in his mind. The taste of her lips, the feel of her body, her soft moans. He'd had a cockstand since the moment he first placed his lips on hers, and he feared he wouldn't have release anytime soon.

He fisted his hands and rose to his feet. He needed to do something, to work off some of his frustration. Of all the people, he knew he shouldn't have touched Kyndra. But she had been a temptation he was powerless to resist. Now that he had a taste of her, he yearned for more. Much more.

His gaze locked with the canyon wall. They would need to know the lay of the land if he were going to get them to the mountain and Eldar's castle. Without another thought, he climbed the sheer rock wall until he could peek over the edge.

There was a chance the canyon would take them to the mountain. Aimery grunted when he spotted the giant bird pecking clothing from the bones of some poor soul. He didn't want to chance being attacked again.

Aimery had expected the realm to be cloaked in blackness.

Yet, as the sun shed its rays on the mountainside, he saw trees with leaves of vivid pink instead of green. A smile pulled at his lips. This was one of the reasons he loved to visit other realms. There was always something different to see.

By the time he climbed down the canyon, Kyndra had awaken. She had removed her cloak, giving him a view of her full breasts. "Did you sleep well?"

"As well as can be expected. My body hurts. Everywhere."

So did his. "Our magic healed us. Without it, we'll feel everything."

"And die that much easier."

The Fae were immortal, but they could be killed. It was their magic that helped to heal them quickly and gave them long life. Without it…anything could happen.

Kyndra brushed the hair from her face with her hand and scrunched up her nose. "Is the bird still out there?"

"Aye. He procured another meal for the time being."

"What's the plan?"

He lifted a brow. "The plan?"

"I saw you climb up and take a look. You must have found something because you aren't frowning." She touched the spot between her brows. "You furrow your brows."

Aimery hadn't realized he did that. It sent a thrill through him that she had noticed. Had their kiss affected her as much as it had him? Had she dreamed of him holding her as she slept? Did she think of him sliding into her heat, thrusting inside her until sweat beaded their skin and she screamed her release?

He took in a shaky breath and turned his back to her. Regardless of how much his body wanted to feel her soft curves beneath him, there was more at stake here than his need. He clenched his jaw and focused his mind on the mountain.

"We follow the canyon as long as we can. I couldn't see much from the ledge, but I think it takes us to the mountain."

There was a rustle of sand as she gained her feet. "I hope

we're that lucky. Of course, there is no telling what is in the canyon."

"True." He turned to face her. "But doesn't the prospect of finding out excite you?"

Her lips parted in a smile. "Oh, aye. It does."

There was no other person he could imagine by his side at that moment. The anticipation shining in her blue eyes was enough to make his heart skip a beat. Kyndra was afraid, but she also loved not knowing what was going to happen. She was made for just this mission. And he had no doubt she would succeed.

He glanced at her bare legs. A scrape ran down the outside of her right leg. "Does it pain you?"

She cocked her hip out and turned her leg so she could see it. "It hurt last night, but it's fine this morn. We should get moving."

"Do you have any other wounds?"

"I'm sure I have several, just as you do. Stop worrying about me, Aimery. I'll let you know if something needs attention."

He watched her walk past him and smiled. He caught up with her but stayed a step behind her. His gaze frequently strayed to the sway of her hips as she walked. He had to fist his hands to keep from reaching out and touching the dark, thick strands of hair that curled at her waist.

"Why did you choose the dragons?" He had wanted to know the answer to that since first laying eyes on her. Her beauty alone would have commanded any man in the realm, including the king.

She shrugged and glanced at him over her shoulder. "Why did you choose to become a commander?"

"I'm good at what I do. I worked my way up through the ranks and proved that I was trustworthy and able to make difficult decisions."

She chuckled. "It didn't hurt that you were friends with the king."

"Theron doesn't choose friends for positions unless they've proven their worth."

She stopped and faced him. "It wasn't my intent to offend you."

"You didn't. I'm merely making a point." He wouldn't let her know that she had offended him. He had worked bloody hard for position of Commander, and he'd be damned to see it made light of.

"Ever since I was a little girl I've dreamed of the dragons. It was never enough to see them flying through the sky, their roars echoing through the night. I wanted to be near them, to know them."

Her face had relaxed into a smile at the mention of the dragons. "They are magnificent creatures."

"They are much more than that. Their beauty, their grace is breathtaking to behold. I've dedicated my life to learning all there is to know of the Blues. I've spent hours gaining their trust so I could venture through the Quay of Skulls and their lairs. No other priestess has ever accomplished that feat."

"And you should be proud of it."

She grinned, her gaze lowering in her embarrassment. "I am. Very much so."

"Because of that feat, you're next in line to be High Priestess of the Dragon Order."

"I am. It's what I've always wanted. Just as you've worked to become Commander of the army, I've worked to be the High Priestess. To be near all the dragons of our realm would be a dream come true."

Aimery started walking again. He couldn't look into Kyndra's swirling blue eyes and not understand about dreams. He'd had a dream for so long now, a dream that had begun to fade and wither…until he had seen Kyndra.

He was tired of being alone, tired of eating and sleeping by himself. He might live in the palace with Theron, but he refused to intrude on their family time. He would be welcome, he knew that, but it wasn't the same. He wanted his own family, to see his wife's welcoming smile when he returned home, to have her arms wrap around him in the night, to see her belly swell with his child.

It was a hard lesson to learn that not all dreams came true. Many got their dreams but, for warriors like him, he was destined to a life of solitude.

"Aimery?"

He glanced at her beside him. "Aye?"

"Are you all right? You got quiet."

"I'm just thinking of Isran."

Kyndra knew he lied, but she let him. Something she had said had disturbed him. She had seen his eyes dim before he had turned away. He was such a mystery. His exploits were known across the realm, but few knew the real man. Kyndra realized then, she wanted to be one of the few who knew him.

She licked her lips and tried to keep up with his long strides. "By your reaction at the Quay of Skulls after you touched the male dragon, I gather Isran was a friend."

"Was."

That one simple word was filled with loathing and retribution. Aimery wasn't a Fae she wanted angry at her for any reason. He was nearly as powerful as Theron, and his vengeance was swift.

"He's the one who committed the murders, isn't he?"

Aimery sighed and nodded.

"I'm sorry. I cannot imagine to know how it feels to be betrayed in such a way."

"I hope you never find out."

"Was he high ranking in the palace?"

"Nay. He was working his way through the ranks of the army, just as I did. I recognized his skill and knew it could be to our benefit."

She grimaced. "So you befriended him."

"Aye. I didn't see him for what he was." He stopped and raked a hand down his face. "My judgment comes into question now. Theron has every right to remove me as

Commander."

"For one mistake?" She couldn't believe it. Surely Theron had more mercy than that.

Aimery's blue gaze settled on her. "Kyndra, I make life and death decisions for my men and our realm. If I make a mistake, we could lose everything."

"You've proven your worth a thousand times over. Have you ever made a mistake before?"

"Not like this."

"Then give Theron some credit to recognize that. Even he has made mistakes by sending his own brother into the Realm of Shadows."

Suddenly, Aimery grinned. "Are you trying to cheer me up."

Kyndra bit the inside of her cheek and shrugged. "Maybe. I just want you to realize that you are worth more to our realm as a Commander than you think."

Her breath stilled in her body as his hand reached up and pulled a lock of her hair from her eyelashes. The need to step into his arms, to feel them wrap around her as she gave in to the desire swimming through her blood, would be so easy, feel so wonderful.

She watched him rub the strand of hair between his long fingers. Her dark locks amid the flaxen-haired Fae had always made her feel different, out of place. Her parents had told her few were granted the gift of dark hair in their race, but Kyndra would have gladly given it to someone else.

But now, as Aimery stroked her hair as if he were mesmerized, she found she liked being different.

"I love your hair," he murmured.

She closed her eyes as he took a step toward her. With her heart hammering in her chest, she waited for him to pull her against him, to claim her lips in another kiss that would set her world on fire.

But he did neither.

She opened her eyes in time to see him drop her hair.

Disappointment filled her, even though she told herself it was for the best.

"It is rare for a Fae to have dark hair," he said. "Though I'm sure you know that."

"I do. It is said to be a great gift, but being so different is more of a curse than a gift."

One side of his mouth lifted in a grin. "Because so many wanted you."

"Only because of my hair. They thought by having me as their wife I would somehow elevate them."

"Is that why you took the vows of the Order?"

She had never told anyone of how she hated having hair so different or of the men chasing her. Everyone thought she had cared more for the dragons than men. It was true. To an extent.

"I took the vows because it was my destiny."

"And it made no never mind to you that by taking them it kept the men from you?" he asked with a raised brow.

She shrugged. "Oh, that might have factored into things."

When he did nothing but stare at her, she shifted from one foot to the other, growing more uncomfortable by the moment.

"With your beauty, you could have ruled the realm, Kyndra. It isn't just the color of your hair, it's your strength, your splendor that brought those men to your door. Hiding behind the dragons won't stop what everyone sees."

"And what is that?" she couldn't help but ask. No one had spoken to her as Aimery did, and it made her stomach flutter.

"You were meant to be adored. And not just by dragons."

Her eyes followed him as he turned and continued down the canyon floor. No one had ever made her doubt her decision to take her vows, until Aimery. He made her think of a future she could never have, because she wanted to be with the dragons always. The dragons were her life, just as the army was his life. He could have both the army and a family.

She couldn't.

Chapter Nine

Kyndra wiped the sweat from her forehead and licked her dry lips. Her stomach rumbled, and thirst clawed at her belly. She glanced up at the sky. At first she had thought it was the sun casting the sky in the orange light, but the higher the sun climbed, the brighter the orange got.

"Is the sky orange here?"

Aimery chuckled. "You're just now noticing that?"

"I've been a little occupied navigating the canyon." The canyon floor had gotten rockier the closer to the mountains they had gotten. She had twisted her ankles more times than she wanted to count, and she became testier with each passing moment.

He held out his hand to her to help her up a large boulder. "Wait until we reach the mountain. The leaves on the trees aren't green but a bright pink."

She narrowed her gaze at him. "Are you jesting with me?"

"You'll see for yourself soon."

She hoped so, because she desperately wanted out of the canyon. The arid temperatures were playing havoc with her.

They walked another half hour when Aimery stopped and cocked his head to the side. "Do you hear that?"

Kyndra moved beside him and listened. After a moment she heard the unmistakable sound of water. She smiled at Aimery. "Is it close?"

"Let's find out."

She never thought twice about taking his hand as he rushed toward the water. Kyndra leapt over small rocks, her excitement growing with each step. When they turned a bend in the canyon, they came to a halt.

"By all that's magical," she whispered.

The scene before her was so beautiful it hurt to look at it. The canyon rose up on either side of them to almost meet overhead, leaving only a sliver to allow light to enter. Water cascaded from the mountain into a pool hollowed out in the canyon floor. The water was so clear she could see the wavy lines in the rock, speaking of centuries of water flowing through it. A single palm tree swayed with the power of the waterfall, its pink fronds dripping with water.

"I told you. Pink."

She looked at Aimery and smiled. "I have to admit, though it is pretty, I prefer our green leaves."

"As do I."

She licked her lips and turned to the water. "Is it safe to drink?"

"Only one way to find out."

She followed him to the water's edge. The rock was a so pale in places it looked almost white. She knelt beside Aimery and fought the urge to dive into the water to cool off. Her boots, perfect for their climate, were sticking to her legs in the arid heat.

"It'll be better in the mountains," he said as if reading her mind.

He cupped his hand in the water and brought it to his lips. Just before he drank, she placed her hand on his arm.

"As thirsty as I am, I'd rather not be in this place alone."

He looked from his hand to her. "It's flowing water, which means it's more than likely all right to drink. I don't smell anything."

Before she could argue more, he brought his hand to his lips and drank. Kyndra waited, her stomach tied in knots.

"It tastes wonderful," Aimery said with a smile.

It was all Kyndra needed to hear. She plunged her hands into the cool water and sighed. She bent and drank deeply, enjoying the feel of the liquid as it quenched her parched throat.

When she finally drank her fill, she sat up to find Aimery leaning against the canyon wall, one leg stretched in front of him, the other bent with his arm resting on his knee. His eyes were closed, but she knew he didn't sleep.

"We're at the base of the mountain," he said. "We can climb out of the canyon and onto the mountain."

She moved across from Aimery, stretching out in the shade. "Or?"

"How did you know there was an 'or'?"

"A guess."

"Or…we can follow the cave behind the waterfall."

Kyndra leaned to the side and looked through the falls. She didn't see a cave but, if Aimery said it was there, she believed him. "Which way would you prefer?"

He cracked open his eyes and shrugged. "Each will hold its own dangers. Inside a cave, we'll be limited to where we can go. Plus, we have no idea if it's a dead end or not."

"And the mountain?"

"If the giant bird is any indication, I think we'll encounter more animals like it. Eldar hasn't held his reign over this realm for this long without reason. There will be guards and traps along the way for us."

"Will the cave?"

"Most likely."

She blew out a breath. "So it doesn't matter does it?"

He shrugged again.

"Then you pick." Aimery had more experience traveling to different realms than she did. She trusted him more than she trusted herself.

"Are you sure?"

"I'm sure."

He sat up and turned so that he looked at the waterfall then lifted his head as if he were thinking of the mountain. "As much as I'd like to stay hidden, I think the cave is a bad idea."

"Then the mountain it is."

He faced her, his mouth in a thin line. "It's going to be dangerous, Kyndra."

"And nothing else has been? I'm ready for whatever we encounter."

"Are you ready for Isran?"

She blinked. "What?"

"My gut tells me we'll face Isran soon. Will it be before we speak to Eldar? I don't know but, regardless, we must be prepared for Isran."

"Isn't the point in coming here to find him? Don't we want to capture him and return to our realm so he can face his punishment?"

Aimery saw the ire rise in her eyes. "You cannot enter someone's realm and take something without asking first."

"Isran stole from us."

"I know. Do you think anyone would come into our realm and leave without first seeking Theron? Nay, they wouldn't, not if they wanted to leave our realm. It's the same here. The only way we'll be able to leave is with Eldar's permission."

"And if Isran has taken over?"

He had also imagined such a possibility. "Then we'll have to fight him."

She blinked. Twice. "Fight him? Fight a Fae who uses black magic when we have no magic of our own? It's a death sentence, Aimery."

"Not if we can get the egg."

She rolled her eyes and got to her feet to pace in front of him. "He won't be fool enough to let the egg out of his sight."

"Nay, he won't chance that."

"The egg is large enough that it will take a couple of men to carry it, especially since Isran can't use his magic."

"I agree."

She stopped and looked at him. "Do you know why he took the egg?"

"For power."

"Power, aye. But do you know what he plans to do with it?"

Aimery shook his head.

"You told me at the palace you knew all there was to know."

"Kyndra, if you know something, tell me."

She sighed. "The egg of a blue dragon is priceless. They lay so few, that to steal one gives the thief credibility."

"I know."

She swallowed and licked her lips, a nervous tick she had. "Just having the egg could give him the men he needs to wrestle power from Eldar."

"You aren't telling me anything I don't already know."

"Then do you know that if he cracks the egg and bathes in the yolk, he will be invincible."

Aimery's stomach fell to his feet. "What?"

"Not many know this benefit to a blue dragon egg."

"That's black magic, though. How do you know it?"

She shrugged. "I found it in a book."

"Good gods." Aimery rose to his feet and fought the rising panic in his chest. He doubted even Theron knew of this probability but, regardless, it changed nothing. "Can he crack the egg at any time?"

"Aye, but once it's cracked, he must use the yolk then or it's forfeited. The egg itself holds immeasurable power. Would Isran use it before, or after, he takes the throne from Eldar?"

Aimery laughed, his frustration mounting. "I don't know. I used to think I knew Isran, but the man I called friend wouldn't have used black magic, and he would never have killed a dragon or stolen an egg."

"Where would a Fae such as Isran hide on this realm?"

That got Aimery's attention. He narrowed his gaze and searched his mind. "Isran can't take over Thav by himself. He will need men."

"Men like we saw in the capital?"

"He wouldn't be fool enough to gather men at the base of Eldar's palace. He would be somewhere farther away from Eldar's prying eyes."

She crossed her arms over her chest. "I'm surprised Eldar hasn't felt the egg's magic."

"Maybe he has. Maybe that's why there were so many guards at the wall last night. Eldar isn't a fool. He knows something is up, which is why we need to get in to see him before Isran makes his move."

"If Isran isn't near here, our chances of getting to see Eldar should be in our favor."

"Should be. Tell me, what exactly happens to Isran if he bathes in the yolk. I know you said he becomes invincible, but everything can be killed."

She shook her head. "Of all the dragons, our blue dragon holds the most magic. Take the purest form of that in the yolk and mix it with black magic. The combination has been whispered about for ages, but no one has ever managed to steal an egg. We don't really know what Isran will become if the yolk touches him."

"Eldar has taken Isran's magic away."

"He's used great amounts of it though. There is no doubt that his power will be greater if he has the use of his black magic."

"He'll have to kill Eldar for that then."

Aimery wanted certainties, but there weren't any. The only thing he could do was hope the idea of more power would prevent Isran from using the yolk until he reached Eldar and the palace.

Chapter Ten

Kendra blew out a breath. "Then it's up to the castle?"

Aimery shrugged. "Maybe."

She wanted to roll her eyes. *Maybe* she mouthed and turned her back to him to look at the pool of water. Her skin was salty from the sweat and caked in dirt, and her hair stuck to the back of her neck making her itch. She palmed the small dagger hidden in the top of her boot and cut a strip of cloth from the bottom of her skirt. As thick and heavy as her hair was, she would be lucky if the material held, but she was willing to chance it if it gave her some relieve from the heat.

Kendra knelt by the pool and splashed water on her face before she combed her fingers through her hair in an effort to untangle the mass before she began to braid it. After she tied off the material to the end of the braid, she let out a sigh.

It was then she realized Aimery hadn't spoken. She looked over her shoulder to find the commander watching her, his blue eyes blazing with a yearning so intense she found herself wanting to go to him.

Her stomach flipped. Many men had looked at her with lust and desire. But none had made her heart pound and her blood heat as Aimery did.

"I was getting hot," she said after a moment.

He swallowed and turned his gaze away. "Don't you find it odd that Eldar hasn't sent guards to find us?"

"Why would he? You said yourself he holds all the power."

"That's true but, if I were him, I would want to know why a Fae had come to my realm."

"Wouldn't the same argument be used for Isran?"

Aimery shrugged his wide shoulders. "Who's to say Eldar didn't send men to look for him? Maybe Isran was able to hide."

"And we don't want to hide. We want to be found."

"Exactly," he said with a grin. "So where are the guards?"

A shiver of apprehension raced down her spine. "I'm not liking this. Not at all."

"Neither am I."

"If only we could have our powers," she started.

"Kyndra, don't."

His gaze bore into hers, alight with a fire she didn't understand. "I just said—"

"I know what you said, but as soon as you start wishing for your powers, you're going to realize what all you could do with them. That's how a Fae goes insane."

She shrugged. "I've felt fine since we came to this awful realm. It hasn't affected me."

"Yet. Don't tempt it. Please."

It was obvious her words had bothered him. They had enough to deal with without adding her insanity on top of everything. "All right."

Aimery pushed away from the wall and moved toward the waterfall to tilt his head back and look at the mountain. "It's midday, I believe."

He had to shout over the roar of the falls, and Kyndra walked closer to him. It had felt as if they had walked the canyon an entire day, not just part of it. "Then we best not waste more time here."

"I agree." He turned to her. "Drink your fill. We should

find water on the mountain, especially if we follow the flow of the river."

"But you aren't sure," she finished for him.

They shared a smile and went to the pool. Kyndra was the first to finish drinking. She sat up and stilled. "Um…Aimery?"

"Hmm?" he murmured while drinking.

"Remember how curious you were about Eldar's guards?"

In an instant Aimery was on his feet, his sword in his hand as he faced six guards. Kyndra glanced behind her and saw three more descending the canyon wall.

"What are you doing on Thav?" demanded a guard.

Aimery lifted a shoulder. "I've come to see, Eldar. I have a private message he'll want to see."

"Give me the message."

Kyndra licked her lips and put her hand on her sword. She had thought the guards would take them to Eldar but, by the way they were acting, they seemed to want a fight.

"As emissary to King Theron of the Realm of the Fae, I demand to see King Eldar," Aimery said.

At once the guards lowered their weapons. "Follow us."

Kyndra walked to Aimery as he put away his sword. "Why didn't you say that to begin with?"

"I wanted to see what they would do," Aimery whispered. "At least we won't have to climb the mountain."

She smiled. "I'm more concerned with finding food."

"I'll make sure you're fed."

And she had no doubt he would.

They followed the guards up the side of the waterfall to a path that was hidden amid the lush foliage that had grown around the water. It was such a stark contrast from the barren canyon that Kyndra found she wanted to enjoy it. The pink leaves intrigued her.

"No time," Aimery whispered in her ear as he took her arm and steered her near him. "Once all this is solved, I'll ask Eldar for a few days so you can explore the mountain."

Kyndra had been on her own, making decisions herself for

so long that it felt…nice…to have Aimery think of her. In the Order, each priestess was responsible for herself and all elders. She had quickly gotten used to the routine, but now she realized what her sister had meant when she told Kyndra it was nice to have someone to share a burden with, someone to help make decisions.

At the time, Kyndra thought her sister weak. But she wasn't weak, she had recognized a solitary life was lonely. Kyndra wasn't lonely. She had her dragons and the other priestesses. Aimery, however, was different. He made her think differently, feel differently.

She should be shocked and wary of such feelings, but instead she found she wanted to explore them more.

The path took them to an entrance in the mountain. As soon as they stepped into the mountain, the cool air surrounded her. Torches lit the way, and the lead guard held one above his head as well.

Aimery's hand on her arm was reassuring, warm. It brought to mind his hands caressing her back as he pressed her against his hard length. Kyndra swallowed as her nipples hardened. She shivered thinking about his hands on her breasts.

"Are you all right?"

Aimery's breath fanned her neck as he leaned near her. His heat was distracting, making her think thoughts she was better off not thinking. "I'm just chilled."

They didn't speak more, and Kyndra forced her mind away from images of licking Aimery's body and stroking his chest. But the flames of desire were already consuming her, making her sex throb and her breasts ache.

Aimery knew something was wrong with Kyndra, but the inadequate light didn't allow him to see her face as he wanted to. Her body was stiff, and her breathing had quickened. Maybe she was afraid of closed spaces. The thought of Kyndra terrified left him with the urge to wrap his arms around her, to hold her close to his body and tell her everything would be all right.

"In here," a guard said.

Aimery guided Kyndra into the lift. He looked up to see the ropes disappear into the darkness it went so high. A board connecting each side of the lift was the only thing separating them from the emptiness below them.

Kyndra leaned on the board and looked over the side. "How far down does this go?"

"Very, far," a guard answered. "Careful lest you fall over."

She righted herself and raised her brows. "And these…ropes…that are holding this…piece of wood…with all of us on it is supposed to take us to the top. Without breaking."

The guard nodded. "We've used it for years."

"My point exactly."

Aimery grinned and turned his face away so Kyndra couldn't see it. The lift frightened her, not that he could blame her. The wood was squishy in places, and the board going around the sides didn't give him the feeling of being safe. Falling had never scared him until now.

He scooted closer to Kyndra so he could grab her if she fell. She gripped the boards, her knuckles turning white as the lift squeaked into motion. Aimery should have been thinking of what he was going to say to Eldar, but he watched Kyndra with a hunger that grew the longer he was with her.

When he caught the guards looking at her with lust in their eyes, it was all he could do not to smash their faces in. Kyndra wasn't for them.

She's not for you either.

It was a fact he knew well enough, but he could fantasize. He'd been doing that since before their first kiss. And after the kiss, after he'd tasted her, his fantasies only increased.

No, Kyndra had chosen the dragons. He would not put her in a position where she had to choose him or her vows, because he knew, though she might like his kiss, he didn't stand a chance against a dragon.

He couldn't deny that, if she gave a hint of wanting him, he would throw caution to the wind and make love to her until they were both too exhausted to move.

Her fingers grazed his leg, causing him to look down at her hand. She had moved closer to him, as if seeking his protection. He could promise her safety, but without his powers his vow was nothing more than words.

He had told her earlier not to speak about the loss of her powers because it had been affecting him more than he liked. All he could think about was how much easier he could protect Kyndra with his magic. He felt the loss of his magic like a kick in his ballocks. And he hated it.

Kyndra, however, seemed to be adjusting well. There were times she fisted her hands as she if she compared their situation to how it would be if she had her magic. Yet she never complained. So far she had kept a level head. Aimery didn't think he could say the same. With the lust burning his blood for her and the frustration of his loss of magic, he was on the raggedy edge. Not a good place to be in their present situation.

"Will it ever end?" Kyndra whispered.

Aimery looked into her eyes, her face in an orange glow from the torch held near her. "Soon enough."

Her brows furrowed and, her fear of the lift forgotten, she placed her hand on his chest as she faced him. "Are you all right?"

Nay. "Aye."

She stood up on tiptoe until her mouth was near his ear. Aimery bit back a groan and fought to keep his hands at his side instead of wrapping around her.

"It's the magic, isn't it? I need you, Aimery. I can't do this alone."

He clenched his jaw and breathed in her scent of jasmine and sunlight. As he parted his lips to answer her, he caught one of the guards giving him a knowing look. Something in Aimery snapped. He stepped toward the guard, causing the lift to rock and Kyndra to yelp in fear.

"Easy, Fae," the guard said.

Aimery leaned until he was nose to nose with the man. "Don't look at her again. Do you understand me?"

The guard nodded, and Aimery returned to his spot beside Kyndra.

"What was that about?" she demanded as she looked from the guard to Aimery.

Aimery's gaze met the guard's before he turned to her. "A small conflict that has been seen to."

She rolled her eyes and turned away from him, but she kept her hand near his. A small sigh escaped her parted lips when the lift began to slow. Aimery's looked away from those plump lips that he imagined sliding over his cock. His rod swelled with a hunger only Kyndra could quench, a hunger that grew with each beat of his heart.

"We've arrived," another guard said.

The lift came to a halt and Aimery stared at the yawning corridor before him, ablaze with light from candelabras hanging from the ceiling and walls. Lining the walls were giant tapestries of vivid colors, the artwork some of the best Aimery had ever seen. Of everything he had imagined Eldar's castle to be, this certainly wasn't it.

He stepped off the lift and held out his hand for Kyndra. Once she was beside him, he heard her gasp as she took in the splendor.

They had made it to Eldar's castle.

Chapter Eleven

Kyndra lounged in the massive bathing tub. It wasn't as nice as what she was used to on her realm, but it was a bath with hot water, which was enough for her. She had washed the sand and sweat from her body three times and washed her hair four times.

She smiled as she thought of Aimery. He had been indignant that Eldar hadn't seen them immediately. The only thing that had calmed Aimery down was Eldar's promise that he would see them in a few hours.

It had been enough for her. The thought of a room to herself with food and a bath had been all she needed to hear. Yet when Aimery had discovered their rooms weren't near each other, she had thought she would have to restrain him herself.

Something had happened to Aimery. She still couldn't believe his reaction on the lift. What had come over him to get in the guard's face, and what had he growled at the man? Kyndra was likely never to know. What she did know was that Aimery wasn't handling the loss of his magic well. He had hid it from her well enough, but she knew.

She knew because she felt it herself.

It would be so easy to give in to the fear and anger at the loss, but she couldn't. She fought it every waking moment. She should have listened to Lugus better, taken to heart his words of caution and control. All she had now was Aimery. The thought of losing him left her gasping for breath.

"Kyndra."

She jerked upright at the sound of his voice in the hallway. "I'm here."

Before she could tell him she was at her bath, the door to her chamber opened, and he stepped inside. She forgot all about her nudity as she looked at him. He wore a tunic of black, accented with cream thread, and black breeches that molded to his muscular legs. His hand was on the hilt of his dagger, and she glimpsed the pommel of his sword over his shoulder. His hair hung loose about his shoulders, the ends still damp.

Then her gaze met his. The stark hunger blazing in his eyes made her heart skip a beat and her stomach flutter. She gripped the tub and started to rise before she knew what she was about. At the last moment, she stopped herself, wishing for the first time since she had become a priestess that she wasn't bound by her vows.

She wanted to touch, Aimery, to kiss him, caress him. Love him. She wanted to feel his hard length against her, to know what it felt like to have him lie atop her, thrusting inside her.

"I wanted to make sure you were all right, that Eldar was treating you well."

Kyndra smiled at his words. He was always thinking of her. "Aye. I've already eaten my fill and then some. I see you have new clothes."

He grimaced and shrugged. "I came out of my bath to find my clothes gone and replaced with these."

"They left your weapons at least."

"Aye." He moved to her bed and chuckled. "Looks as though you'll be wearing something new as well."

Kyndra sat back in the water, letting it cover her breasts.

She should be ashamed to have Aimery with her as she bathed, but it made her feel decadent and aroused. "I admit it is odd to see you wear anything other than blue, silver and white."

"Do you not like the black?"

She liked it a lot. Too much. "It looks good on you."

He glanced at the bed. "I cannot wait to see you in this gown."

"What color is it?" Part of her was hoping it was black as well. She'd never worn such a color. To a Fae, black signified evil and death. Yet, seeing it on Aimery, watching how the tunic moved across his thick chest and arms made her appreciate the hue anew.

"You'll see."

The water began to cool, but she was hesitant to get out with Aimery in her room. Yet she didn't want him to leave. How she had become so mixed up she wasn't sure. Aimery turned her about, kept her off kilter until she forgot everything but him.

Before she changed her mind, she stood and reached for the towel. She was too embarrassed to meet his gaze, but she felt his eyes on her. She wrapped the towel around her and walked to the bed and the gown that waited for her.

"Cream," she said and touched the soft material. The gown was simple in its elegance and so different from anything she had ever worn. "I like it."

"I want to see you in it."

The harsh croak of Aimery's words jerked her gaze to him. If she had thought his gaze burned her before, she might go up in flames now. There was no doubt he wanted her. How she wished he would take her in his arms and kiss her again. She wanted him with a desperation that frightened her.

But she didn't want to have to choose him.

If he took her, she could always say it had been the loss of her magic that had made her turn to him. Though she knew that wasn't fair to Aimery, it was the only way she could have what she wanted.

He walked to her and lifted a wet strand hair from her shoulder. He leaned toward her, his mouth near her ear. "Don't go anywhere without me," he whispered. "I don't trust Eldar."

She forgot to breathe as he turned his head until their mouths were breaths apart. All she had to do was lean forward to touch his lips with hers, to feel again the thrill of his kiss, the way he made her body throb with desire.

But she couldn't do it.

"I'll be right outside your chamber," he said before he turned on his heel and left.

Kyndra waited until the door closed behind him before she let out her breath she'd been holding. If ever there was someone who could make her throw away everything she had worked toward, it was Aimery.

All Fae were sensual creatures, but Aimery held an essence of wildness about him, a streak of uncertainty that called to her on a level she hadn't experienced before. And, oh, how she wanted to experience more of the thrill that raced through her whenever he was near.

With a sigh of regret, Kyndra dropped her towel and reached for her new clothes.

Aimery leaned his head against Kyndra's door and cursed himself for ten kinds of fool. What kind of idiot stayed in her chamber when she was bathing? It was an enticement he didn't need, one he couldn't ignore. Every fiber of his being told him to leave, but his mind couldn't make his body work.

Instead, he had soaked up her beauty. Her hair was slicked against her head from the recent rinsing, and beads of water clung to her skin as if they desired her as much as he did. When she had risen from the tub, the glimpse of her body had made him break into a cold sweat. Ripe, full breasts that tapered to a narrow waist and flared hips to her long, luscious legs that he wanted wrapped around his waist as he buried his cock inside her.

She had surprised him by getting out of her bath, and few people did that.

He needed to tell her to stay with him, to be careful, but when he had whispered in her ear, he had smelled her fragrance of jasmine and sunshine, and all thought fled. Then, she had met his gaze, her lips parting.

She had wanted his kiss. Of that he was sure. Yet, he couldn't do it. He knew deep in his soul that if he took Kyndra, he could never let her go. And if she accepted him, it would only be for a moment in time.

One or the other would be hurt if they gave in to the desire. Which is why he intended to stay strong and resist her lure.

Aimery blew out a breath and forced his attention away from Kyndra to Eldar. He had managed to hide Theron's missive with his weapons that he kept near him while he bathed. He wouldn't put it past Eldar to try and take his weapons as well. They were so near to gaining a great advantage over Isran that Aimery could hardly contain himself. It was eating away at him that he had to wait to speak to Eldar. All the time wasted, when they could have readied the castle.

He paced the hall in front of Kyndra's chamber. At least he had managed to have their rooms near each other. Eldar had wanted him across the castle from Kyndra, but Aimery refused. Time crawled at a snail's pace until Kyndra's door opened and she stepped through.

Aimery was struck anew at how stunning she was. Her dark curls, unadorned, floated about her shoulders. The cream gown hung to her slippered feet and hugged her slim frame. The material was gathered at her shoulders and held together by gold bands. The front draped becomingly down her front, giving a hint of the swell of her breasts.

He smiled and motioned her forward. Then stopped dead in his tracks as he stared at the back of the gown. She turned her head to look at him over her shoulder, and his balls tightened. The gown bared her back with the material draping below her waist, giving any one who looked a glimpse of her hip.

"Isn't it lovely?" she asked and spun around. "I feel...wicked."

She looked good enough to eat. Aimery licked his lips. "No man will be able to keep his eyes from you."

"Just because of what I'm wearing?"

"Whether you know it or not, men watch you. In that gown, they'll devour you."

She tilted her head to the side and regarded him. "Has a woman ever held such power over you before?"

Only you. "Nay."

"Maybe it will help us convince Eldar."

Aimery grunted and walked to her. "Only if you want to become his concubine."

She shivered and fell in step beside him. "I'd rather not."

"I didn't think so. Just make sure we are always together. Don't leave your chamber with anyone but me."

"I am a warrior, Aimery. I can take care of myself."

"You haven't seen what they do to women they take captive, Kyndra. If they want a woman, whether she wants to go or not, they will have her."

Her steps faltered. "Should I wait in my chamber?"

"Nay." Aimery steadied her with a hand on her back. As soon as he touched her bare skin, he wished he hadn't. Her skin was soft, warm, and he wanted to feel more of her. "Whatever happens, stay with me."

"I don't have my weapons. I didn't even think."

"That's what Eldar wanted you to do. Few women can pass up a beautiful gown, even one where wearing their weapons is impossible. If it comes down to it, I'll toss you one of mine. Stay alert."

She nodded. "Where are we going?"

"To the great hall. We're to stay there until Eldar summons us."

The music he had heard whispering through the castle grew louder the closer to the great hall they ventured. Guards were placed at every entrance, and Aimery was sure if he tried to go anywhere but the great hall they would be stopped.

He and Kyndra followed the corridor down several flights of stairs to another hallway. The beat of the music filled the castle, echoing off the stones. The music was soft, erotic, as it washed over him.

"Aimery," Kyndra murmured as she leaned against him. "The music. It has magic in it."

"I know."

He stopped her before they entered the great hall. "Be careful, Kyndra. For me."

She swayed with the music before she rose up on her toes and placed her lips against his. "I'm glad you're with me."

Chapter Twelve

Aimery held himself still, the feel of Kyndra's soft curves brushing against him was the worst kind of torture. She ended the kiss with a seductive smile before she turned her back to him. His gaze lingered on the small of her back where the cream material of her gown moved with her skin, tantalizing him, urging him to brush his fingers against the spot.

He took in a calming breath and followed Kyndra into the great hall and down the long rows of tables. Fortunately, she sat near the end, leaving the end seat for him. He slid onto the stool and gazed at the abundance of food that covered the table. From whole roasted boar, various birds, boiled potatoes and cabbage, fruit and bread, it was a feast for a king.

Kyndra licked her lips. "I thought I was full, but I find the smell divine."

Aimery had to admit the food smelled delicious, and he couldn't wait to get a piece of the boar. The magic was lulling him, taking his worries away. He fought against it and, when that didn't work, all he had to do was look at Kyndra.

She smiled at him, her swirling blue eyes heavy lidded as she swayed on her seat. A lock of hair fell over her eye, the curl stopping near her lips. Aimery tucked the strand behind her ear and let his fingers graze the smooth skin of her jaw.

"Dance with me," she whispered.

Aimery shook his head. He dared not hold her in his arms. The music was too erotic, the pull too great to ignore. His cock throbbed with need, begging him to take Kyndra. He wouldn't allow them to be put in a situation where she woke the next morning aghast at what they had done.

"Please, Aimery. I cannot fight the music."

With the way other men were staring at her, Aimery knew if he didn't dance with her, someone else would. There was no way he was allowing any other man to touch her. Not his Kyndra.

"One dance."

Her eyes sparkled as she smiled. "One dance."

Aimery got to his feet and held out his hand. As soon as Kyndra placed her palm in his, heat stole up his arm and surrounded his body. The music was slow, steady, the beat of the drums rhythmic and captivating. The notes of a flute floated through the air and accompanied the haunting strings of the violin.

He held out his hands and groaned when Kyndra's body pressed against his. The feel of her full breasts made his balls tightened, but it was her parted lips and closed lids that caught him in her spell.

Their bodies swayed as one, giving in to the seductive, erotic music. Magic flowed over them, between them…through them.

Aimery could feel his defenses crumbling. His hands spread over Kyndra's bare back, her skin beckoning him to touch more, take more. He caressed a finger down her spine, stopping just short of her buttocks. She shivered and let out a breathy moan. He pulled her against him and buried his head in her neck, inhaling her sweet scent.

"Aimery," she whispered as her fingers threaded through his hair.

His heart pounded. His blood boiled. His hands shook from

the effort to keep from ripping the gown from her body and laying her on the table so he could plunge inside her regardless of the crowded hall and the eyes that watched them. How he wanted to feel her clenching around his rod, to hear her scream her release. He cared about nothing else but her, Kyndra, the woman who had invaded his mind.

"Kiss me." Her lips teased his ear. "I want to taste you again."

It would be so easy to give in, to take what she offered. But he couldn't. He pushed against the magic and the music and loosened his arms from Kyndra. When he stepped away from her, her brows furrowed.

"Aimery?"

He took another step back. "I can't do this. You'll regret this later."

"I won't."

But he knew she would. If he took her, claimed her virginity, her vows would be forsaken. Everything she had strived for with the dragons would be gone. She would hate him then, hate the very sight of him.

"You want it now but only because of the magic."

She shook her head, her dark curls catching the light of the torches. "You don't understand."

"I do. Please, Kyndra. I'm holding on by a thread."

And that thread was quickly unraveling.

He had to get away from her, to leave the music. He needed time to get his mind and body back under control. "I'll be back," he said and turned on his heel.

Kyndra watched Aimery leave with a sinking heart. She had finally made the decision to give in to her desires, and Aimery didn't want her. At least he said he didn't want her, but she had felt his rod, hard and thick, against her.

Whatever the future held for her, she knew one thing for certain—she had to have Aimery. She would never forgive herself if she didn't taste the temptation he offered. Without another thought, she lifted her skirt and hurried after him.

Once through the double doors, she stopped and looked first one way then the other of the corridor. It was only by chance that she saw a shadow move. She knew instantly it was Aimery. Kyndra lifted her chin and followed him.

He wandered aimlessly, unaware she was behind him. Many times he would stop and brace his hands against the wall, his head bent forward as if the weight of the realms rested on his shoulders.

Tears pricked her eyes when she heard him whisper her name. She could stand it no more. Her feet made nary a sound as she approached him. When she was steps away his head jerked up, their gazes meeting.

"What are you doing here?" he demanded as he straightened.

"What I should have done earlier." Kyndra walked to him and rose up on her tiptoes as her arms slid around his neck.

His hands grasped her arms. "Kyndra. Nay."

"Aimery, I'm tired of fighting this desire for you. I know what you're trying to do, but I want this. I want this more than anything else in the realms. Please. Make love to me."

It was as if her words had burst through his walls. His arms wrapped around her tightly, molding her to his body as his mouth slanted over hers. Again and again he kissed her until she was breathless and aching for more.

He pulled back and took her hand. "Not here."

Kyndra blinked, her gaze blurry from the desire. She managed to lift her skirts before she tripped on them while Aimery pulled her to his chamber. Excitement pooled in her belly, making her heart beat faster.

He slammed and bolted the door before he turned to her. "Last chance."

She could say all the right words, and still he wouldn't believe her. There was only one thing she knew she could do that would prove to him she really did want him. She reached her hands on to her shoulders and unclasped the gold bands. Her gown fluttered to her feet, leaving her completely bare.

He growled and in two steps had her in his arms. Kyndra couldn't get enough of his kisses. Her hands yanked up his tunic, eager to feel his skin against hers. Aimery broke the kiss long enough to jerk off his tunic and toss it to the floor.

Before he could claim her mouth again, Kyndra knelt at his feet and pulled off his boots. She looked up at him and rose to her knees. Her hand ran along the length of his rod, feeling his heat through his breeches. His breathing quickened, and his eyes darkened. Her fingers fumbled as she tried to unlace his breeches.

His hands covered hers, stilling her fingers. Slowly, he pulled her to her feet. Kyndra's hands braced against his chest as his fingers caressed her sides. The hunger in his gaze only fanned the flames of her desire. Her eyes closed when his hands cupped either side of her face.

"So beautiful," he whispered. "It hurts just to look at you."

He kissed her jaw, her cheek before placing his lips on her. His tongue flicked out and licked her lips. She wanted a deeper kiss, but he pulled away. Fearing that he might have changed his mind, Kyndra's eyes flew open to find him removing his breeches. Her lips parted in awe as she stared at his cock that sprung free.

She wanted to touch it, to learn every inch of him. But when she took a step to him, Aimery clasped her hands in his. Her back hit the wood of the door as he lifted her arms above her head, their fingers intertwining. He nuzzled her neck, his tongue and lips doing delicious things to her body.

"I'm dreaming," he said.

"Nay. This is real." Any more words were halted when he ground his hips against her.

The feel of his rod against her, free from any clothes, was more delectable than she could have imagined. He slanted his mouth over hers, taking her in a kiss that sizzled with need and an unquenchable hunger.

Her knees buckled from the force of the desire humming through her, but Aimery was quick to catch her. He lifted her in his arms and carried her to the bed. She stared into his eyes, wishing the night would never end.

The cool linen of the sheets met her heated skin. Dimly, she heard the strains of the music below, as if reminding her of its heady pull. Aimery's flaxen hair fell across her breasts as he leaned over her. Kyndra plunged her hands into the silky mass and sighed.

The first touch of his hands on her breasts made her gasp. When he circled her aching nipples with his thumb, heightening her pleasure, she moaned, begging for more. And then his lips closed over a tiny bud.

A strangled cry of rapture passed through her lips. While his tongue and mouth suckled one nipple, his fingers teased and tweaked her other. The throbbing of her sex intensified, urging her to seek more. She shifted her hips, grinding against him. The explosion of pleasure that one movement caused had her doing it again and again, each time the throbbing grew, consuming her.

Aimery was in heaven. Kyndra's beautiful, soft body was beneath his, her moans of ecstasy ringing in his ears. He shifted from one nipple to the other, feasting upon her tender, delectable flesh. Each time she raised her hips to him, he fought to keep from sinking into her heat. She was everything he had ever wanted, ever dared to dream about. He wanted her first time to be something she would never forget, something she could look back on with fondness, even if she despised him. For Aimery knew, despite her words, she would hate him.

He would have this one night to relive in his dreams for the rest of his life. And he intended to make it a night never be forgotten.

Aimery ran his hand over her flat stomach to the soft flare of her hips. His fingers parted the dark curls of her sex before he caressed her sensitive flesh. She moaned when his finger touched her pearl, and he smiled.

He glanced up at her to see her eyes closed and her lips parted. Her pulse beat wildly at her neck as her chest rose and fell rapidly. He groaned when he felt how wet she was and slipped a finger inside her.

His cock jumped when she arched her back and whispered his name. Her arms fell to her side and she fisted the blanket in her hands. Aimery's blood pounded in his ears as he fought the rush of longing. He kissed the spot between her breasts and licked down her stomach before nipping at her navel. She hissed in a breath.

Aimery settled between her legs and kissed first one hip then the other before he turned his attention to her sex. She opened her legs for him when he pushed them wider. He ran his tongue along her sex, tasting her, before he teased her pearl.

She cried out, her back arching again. Her every reaction sent his blood burning through him, making his hunger grow until he was blinded with it. He didn't know how much longer he could hold on before taking her.

He moved his tongue over her pearl with the slightest of touches as he pinched her nipple. She screamed his name and thrashed her head back and forth.

"Aimery, please. I need you."

He could no more ignore the plea than he could ignore his own heart. He rose over her, his cock sliding against her sex. She gripped his back and returned his gaze.

"Now, Aimery," she said and pulled him toward her.

He clenched his jaw as he slid into her wet heat. He tried to move slow, to get her accustomed to him before he breached her maidenhead, but she had her own ideas. She wrapped her legs around him and dug her heels in his buttocks. Every time he plunged into her, she lifted her hips and met his thrusts. He pushed through her barrier before he was ready, and he stilled instantly.

The only sign she gave was a small intake of breath, then she smiled up at him. "Don't stop. It feels too good."

Aimery leaned down and kissed her as he began to move, with long, slow thrusts. He could feel his climax building swiftly, but he refused to peak without her. He increased his tempo, their bodies glistening with sweat.

Suddenly, she whispered his name and jerked as her orgasm claimed her. Aimery continued to thrust, wanting to prolong her pleasure as long as he could, but the feel of her clenching around him sent him over the edge. He threw back his head and gave one final thrust that buried him to the root.

The feel of Kyndra's arms wrapping around him as he spilled his seed inside her was a memory he would never forget.

Chapter Thirteen

Kyndra loved the feel of Aimery's weight on her. He was still inside her, pulsing. And she reveled in it. Her lids drifted close, but she fought the sleep. She wanted to touch him as he had touched her, to learn what pleased him, what made him call out in pleasure.

And she wanted him inside her again.

He slid out of her and rolled onto his back, pulling her with him as he did. She nestled against him, her head on his chest. She couldn't stop smiling. Nothing had ever felt so wonderful, and she wondered how she could have gone so long without experiencing such bliss. Now that she had, however, there was no going back.

She ran her fingers over the valleys and ridges of his chest, marveling in his magnificent form. The arm wrapped around her smoothed the hair away from her face, sending her heart skidding at the simple gesture.

"Aren't you tired?"

She grinned and tilted her face until she looked into his eyes. "A little."

"I obviously didn't wear you out enough."

The teasing glint in his eyes made her stomach flutter.

"You're not done for the night are you?"

"Just getting started. I was just giving you some rest."

"I don't want rest tonight."

His brow furrowed for a moment. "What do you want, Kyndra?"

"I've already told you." She rose up until her face was even with his. "You're all I want."

The vulnerability she saw for a heartbeat in his gaze sent her reeling. She didn't want what had happened between them to be just for the night, but she had assumed that's what it would be. Could he want more? Would he want more?

His hands came up on either side of her face, smoothing back her hair. "Kyndra."

She put a finger to his lips. "Shh. No more talking."

She wasn't going to let him regret what they had done. She is the one who had pushed him into their liaison, and she didn't regret it. Not now, not ever. It had been one of the best decisions of her life, even if it did ruin her chances of being High Priestess. What she got in return outweighed that.

Yet, there was no denying she would miss the dragons.

"We need to talk," Aimery argued.

"Not now. Later."

"There might not be a later."

She kissed him, hoping it would stop his words. Instead, he gripped her shoulders. Kyndra, I'm serious."

She sat back, leaning against his leg he had propped up. "I know you are. What do you want to say? That you regret it?"

"Nay."

"Then what?"

"I don't think you've realized what you've done."

But she did. "I do."

He shook his head. "You can't possibly, not now. Once we return to our realm—"

"If we return."

"Kyndra..." He squeezed his eyes shut and swallowed. When he looked at her again, she saw his anguish, his determination. "I'm responsible for your life."

"I'm not one of your men. I'm the one responsible for my life, Aimery. We are in this together."

He cupped her face and opened his mouth as if he would say more.

"The magic of the dragons might have been taken from us, but you gave me a different kind of magic, a magic I hadn't known existed." She ran a finger down his chest to his flaccid rod and wrapped her hand around him.

She watched, amazed, as he grew hard before her eyes. Her gaze jerked to his.

"This is what you do to me," he said.

It was a power she had never experienced before, and she wasn't about to let it go without exploring more of it. She leaned down to lick and kiss across his chest while her hand explored his length. He grew even longer, harder with each stroke of her hand. Touching wasn't just enough. She wanted to see him, taste him.

Kyndra moved between his legs. She glanced up to find him watching her, the hunger in his eyes spurring her desire. He jerked in her hand, and she looked down to find his head swollen and purple. He was hot and smooth, deliciously hard. Her sex throbbed, eager to have him fill her again, to feel him thrusting hard and fast into her.

She swallowed past a wave of desire and squeezed her legs together. A jolt of pleasure spasmed through her. She leaned down and licked the head of his rod, tasting herself on him. He moaned and clenched the covers.

Kyndra parted her lips and took him in her mouth. He breathed her name, his gaze locked with hers as she ran her lips up and down his length, taking him deeper each time. His gaze darkened with desire, urging her on. She cupped his sacs, rolling them in her hand.

His arms strained as he pulled the blankets, as if he were doing everything he could not to move. Kyndra liked the taste of him, the feel of him in her hands. His hips began to move in time with her. He was fast approaching his climax, and she gloried in the fact she could bring him to it.

The next thing she knew, Aimery had a hold of her and lifted her away from him. He planted her on her hands and knees. Kyndra tried to turn around, but he stopped her with a hand on her back.

"You've brought me to the peak. It's my turn."

Kyndra gasped as he slid into her from behind. Her body stretched to accommodate his length as his arms wrapped around her waist, and he pumped inside her. She looked over her shoulder at him, wanting to tell him how wonderful he felt. Instead, his lips met hers.

She returned his kiss, moaning into his mouth when his hand cupped her breast and rolled her nipple between two fingers. The incredible throbbing began to grow, consuming her. She knew it wouldn't be long before she peaked again. Aimery knew just where to touch her, just how to touch her to make her body come alive.

"Kyndra," he whispered, the sound a loving caress.

His hand moved to her sex and stroked her pearl. She bit her lip as pleasure surrounded her. He plunged faster, harder into her as he stroked.

He nuzzled her ear. "Come for me."

His words sent a shiver of delight through her. With his next thrust, she screamed his name, her body convulsing as waves upon waves of pleasure engulfed her, pulling her down into an abyss of ecstasy.

She held herself up on shaky arms as Aimery gripped her hips and thrust deep inside her. He gave a strangled moan, and then his cock jerked as his seed spilled into her. Tears gathered in her eyes as emotion welled within her.

Aimery fell to his side and pulled her back against him, his body molding around hers. He moved her hair and kissed her neck beneath her ear. "We've got some talking to do in the morn."

This time when her eyes drifted shut, she didn't fight it.

She was in Aimery's arms, safe, sheltered. Nothing could hurt her now.

Chapter Fourteen

Aimery's eyes flew open. He shook his head to clear it from sleep and reached for Kyndra. Only to find the bed empty. He jerked upright and looked at the foot of the bed to find Isran smiling at him.

"Looking for her?" Isran pointed over his shoulder.

Aimery's blood ran cold when she saw Kyndra bound and gagged, the men ogling her nude body as they held her. Rage erupted in him. He leapt from the bed, ready to kill Isran with his bare hands if need be.

Isran smiled, his hands clasped behind his back. His white robes billowed behind him as he walked around Aimery. "The mighty Fae Commander has a weakness. I would never have guessed but, with just one look at the lovely priestess, I can see why."

Aimery held himself in check. He kept himself from looking at Kyndra to control his fury. He couldn't believe he had been so wrapped up in tasting her luscious body that he had forgotten Eldar and their mission. His lack of control could very well end it all.

He faced Isran, uncaring about his own lack of clothing. "Leave Kyndra alone. It's me you want."

"Oh, that's for sure." Isran stopped in front of him and lifted his brows. "It was so easy to fool you. I worried, you know. Everyone spoke about the amazing Aimery, the Fae who battled ancient evil not only on our realm, but Earth as well. The Fae who had ended the reign of the evil, killing off realms one by one."

"I never took credit for any of that. It wasn't just me, but the Fae army and magnificent warriors from Earth and other realms."

"I know. I did enough research on you to know everything, except your weakness. Up until a few hours ago, I didn't think you had a weakness. It was a battle I was looking forward to."

Aimery clenched his fists. "If it's a battle you want, I'll give you one."

"Without your powers?" Isran rolled his eyes and tisked. "I think not."

"Then give me back my powers."

"I'm not a fool, Aimery."

"You're the one using black magic. What have you got to lose?"

Isran smile slowly, his gaze calculating. "You actually want to test your magic against my black magic? You know you could never win. Black magic is many times more powerful than Fae magic."

"Then fight me."

Isran's gaze slid from him to Kyndra then back to Aimery. "I'm surprised you hadn't spoken to Eldar. You were in his castle, eating his food, making use of his...bed."

The frustration that sliced through Aimery cut deep. He alone would carry the burden of his failure. There was no doubt in his mind he would never leave Thav alive, but he would avenge his mistake. He would kill Isran if it was the last thing he did.

"Did you think you had more time?" Isran walked to Kyndra and ran a finger between her breasts. "Did you think I wouldn't move as quickly as I could because I knew Theron would send you? I just hadn't counted on the priestess."

Kyndra fought against her captors, her eyes narrowed on Isran as if she could strike him dead by a look alone. Aimery's heart swelled with pride. Isran had no idea she was a warrior, and if Kyndra could get them off guard she could gain control of the situation.

Out of the corner of his eye Aimery saw the flash of sapphires from the Kyndra's arm cuff. He hadn't remembered her taking it off, but it had been the last thing on his mind last eve. He took a step toward Isran, kicking the cuff beneath the bed. "Where's the egg?"

"You needn't worry about the egg," Isran said and smelled a lock of Kyndra's hair. He released the strand and took in a deep breath. "The egg is safe, somewhere you can never get it."

"Are you sure of that?"

"I'd stake my life on it."

Aimery grinned. "Just what I wanted to hear."

"Take her."

The men holding Kyndra started out the door. Aimery lunged for them but was stopped by four men. No matter how he fought, he couldn't get free. Without his power, he was useless. Despair threatened to swallow him. He longed for his magic, yearned for it as he yearned for breath.

"Kyndra!"

Kyndra blinked back her tears as Aimery bellowed her name. They had been such fools giving in to their passion instead of seeking Eldar, but then that was exactly what Isran had wanted. She had been so drunk with desire, she hadn't realized someone had come into their chamber until she had been yanked out of Aimery's arms.

No matter how much she had fought, she hadn't been able to get free. The gag had gone into her mouth before she'd had a chance to scream Aimery's name, and then they had bound her hands. She had watched, horrified, as Aimery had woken and found her gone. The wild, fierce look in his eyes had sent chills down her spine.

But worse than that was him being adamant at fighting Isran. There was no way Aimery could survive, even with his magic. Black magic was much more powerful, and now that Isran had the dragon's egg...

"Maybe we should have a go at her, aye, Milar," the guard said over her head.

Her ire rose. Bound or not, she wasn't going to allow them to touch her.

Milar laughed. "Oh, aye, Joby. I can't wait to feast on those tits."

The urge to ram her elbow in Joby's nose was strong, but she held herself still. It was no use escaping now, not when she had no idea where she was or what was happening to Aimery.

At least Isran hadn't used the egg. She wasn't sure what was stopping him, but it gave her and Aimery time to get free and think of something.

But what? With no magic what do you think you can do?

The anguish at the loss of her magic threatened to pull her under, to take her to a place where she would no longer worry about it.

She jerked her head to clear her mind. She refused to go insane. She had to stay focused for the Fae realm, for Aimery. She would not abandon him to do their mission alone.

Aimery.

She hadn't gotten to tell him how much she loved their night together, how it would stay in her memories for the rest of her life. She hadn't been able to talk to him about their future, if they even had one. There had been so much she wanted to say. She had gone to sleep imagining how she would wake in the morning and make love to him again.

How had Isran conquered Eldar? How had they not known?

And then she realized—the music. The magical music had ensured they were occupied, leaving Eldar to Isran to do as he pleased.

Kyndra couldn't believe they hadn't realized it at the time, but there was no use crying about it now. Too much was at stake to lie down and wallow in her own self-pity. Now she just had to find out what Isran planned to do with Aimery.

Her feet were numb from the cold stones by the time they reached the chamber. It was three stories down and on the opposite side of Aimery. The guards shoved her inside. Kyndra landed on her hands and knees, scraping them on the stones. She looked over her shoulder at the men advancing on her.

"We'll show ye what a real man can do," Joby sneered, showing blackened teeth and foul breath.

Milar jerked Kyndra onto her back. She kicked out with her foot and connected with Joby's stomach. He bellowed and backhanded her with a meaty fist. The room spun as Kyndra fought to stay conscious.

Joby slapped her again before he jerked open her legs and palmed her breasts. "Aye, yer mine now."

A wave of dizziness washed over Kyndra. She tried to kick out, but Joby only hit her again. The left side of her face was on fire, throbbing with pain. She was powerless to do anything as Joby unlaced his breeches.

"Hurry," Milar said. "I want my turn."

"What is going on here?"

Kyndra didn't think she would ever be so happy to hear Isran's voice. She cracked open her eyes to see him scowling down at her.

"Answer me, Joby. What do you think you're doing?"

Joby licked his lips and shrugged. "Just havin' some fun."

"I told you she wasn't to be harmed. You hit her. Several times. And you were about to rape her."

Joby opened his mouth to argue when he grasped his throat and started choking. Blood bubbled from his mouth and ran down his chin. A heartbeat later he fell to his side, his lifeless eyes staring at the wall.

"Milar," Isran said.

Milar jumped to his feet. "Don't kill me."

Kyndra rolled to her side and curled into a ball. She didn't feel sorry for Joby. The bastard had gotten what he deserved. As far as she was concerned, the same fate could befall Milar as well.

Isran grunted. "Get Joby out of this castle. Let it be a lesson to you. You'll do as ordered, or suffer the consequences."

"Thank you," Millar murmured and stumbled in his effort to get away. He took Joby's arm and dragged him from the chamber.

Kyndra tried to turn away when Isran squatted beside her, but he held her still. He tore off her gag and tossed it aside. "How bad are you hurt?"

"I'll be fine."

"Without your magic, you will feel more pain and take longer to heal. You think you're all right, but you're not. You're body isn't use to this type of pain." To her surprise, he took off his white cloak and draped it over her.

"Why are you being so nice?"

He shrugged. "I have a feeling I'm going to have need of you to help me control Aimery. I don't want to kill him."

"Why?"

"I might want power, Kyndra, but that doesn't mean I can't see a magnificent warrior when I meet one. There hasn't been a Fae like Aimery ever, and we might never see another again. To kill him would be...wrong."

Kyndra wasn't sure if she believed him. However, he had kept her from being raped, and she would do whatever was needed to keep Aimery alive. "He won't rest until he fights you."

Isran sighed and briefly closed his eyes. "I know. He won't stand a chance of winning, either. You're his weakness, Kyndra, the one thing I have he will do anything for."

She bit her tongue as a wave of bittersweet remorse washed over her. She had never wanted to be Aimery's weakness. She had just wanted to be his lover. Surely Isran was wrong.

Isran pulled a dagger from his waist and cut the bonds binding her wrists before sheathing the weapon. "Come. I'll take you somewhere more comfortable."

She didn't fight him when he lifted her in his arms. "You're wrong," she said as he walked from the chamber.

"About what?"

"Me being Aimery's weakness. No woman has ever been his weakness."

One side of Isran's mouth lifted in a smile. "I've seen Aimery with women, Kyndra. I was one of his closest friends. Few women turned his head, and even fewer kept his attention. I've never seen him look at a woman as he looks at you." His gaze met hers. "The hunger in Aimery's gaze is absolute. "

Isran couldn't be right. Kyndra tried to take in a breath and couldn't. She refused to believe she would be the one thing that could destroy Aimery.

"You can save him," Isran said. "Remember that."

She kept her gaze on her hands that clutched his cloak around her. "What makes you think I want to?"

"Because you have the same look in your eyes."

Was she that obvious? She knew she lusted after Aimery, but it couldn't be more than that, could it? The emotions filling her were too new to fully understand.

"I'll do my best to keep him alive," Isran vowed. "Right now he's battling himself to stay sane."

"You shouldn't have taken me from him."

"I need to know how far he will go to get to you."

Kyndra looked at Isran. Was this the same Fae who had stolen a dragon egg and killed a blue dragon? The same Fae who dove into black magic in an effort to take over Thav?

"You control Thav now?"

He nodded. "As of last night. Eldar was much easier to topple than I had anticipated. The magic he had to use in order to take away everyone else's magic aged him to a wrinkled old man."

"You don't plan to make the same mistake?"

Isran chuckled. "Nay. The only one who could have come close to matching me in my power was Lugus before he gave it all up and sacrificed his immortal soul. Now, there is no one. Once I use the dragon egg, no one will dare."

Kyndra took in slow, steady breaths as the pain in her face began to double. Each step Isran took was as if someone were hitting her again.

"Sleep, Kyndra," he whispered.

She tried to keep her eyes open because she needed to know where he was taking her, but his magic was too strong. No longer could she hold off the darkness that pulled at her.

Chapter Fifteen

Aimery had screamed Kyndra's name so many times his throat ached but, with every moment that ticked by and he didn't hear or see her, he knew Isran had killed her. His rage grew, and with Aimery's rage was the need for his magic. He knew he was spiraling into insanity, but it didn't matter. Nothing mattered without Kyndra.

"Kyndra!" He took in several deep breaths, pulling against the shackles that chained him to the wall. "Kyndra!"

He glanced at the bed and the crumpled sheets where they had lain just hours before. Her body had been a taste of paradise, her lips the sweetest nectar. She had been the woman he had longed to find, the woman he yearned to share his life with.

The door to his chamber opened. He craned his neck to the side, praying it was Kyndra. Isran stepped into his line of vision and leaned against the wall, his arms folded over his chest.

"You've been making a lot of noise."

"What did you do with Kyndra?" Aimery demanded.

"She's safe."

Aimery jerked against his chains. "Where. Is. She?"

Isran pushed off the wall and walked toward Aimery. "She's resting. There was, ah…a small misunderstanding with the men who took her."

"What happened?" The thought of Kyndra hurt was like a knife to his belly. The fact he hadn't been there to help her was even worse.

"The men have been dealt with. As for Kyndra, there will be no lasting harm."

"She doesn't have any magic! She can't heal herself."

"But I can," Isran said softly. "And I did. It was minor, Aimery. The man struck her across the face."

Aimery squeezed his eyes closed. *Kyndra. Ah, gods, I'm sorry.*

"Don't you care what I'm going to do with you?"

Aimery's gaze flew open. "I don't give a horse's arse what you do with me. Just let Kyndra go. Free her, and I will spare your life."

Isran's head cocked to the side. "You really believe you can kill me?"

"Without a doubt."

"Even as your mind slips into insanity because you hunger for your magic so?"

Aimery hated that Isran knew what tortures he was going through, but there could be no help for it.

"I'll tell you a secret," Isran said as he moved closer. "I have a better use for you than death."

"I considered you a friend, Isran. A man I called brother. Yet you murdered your own kind and slew a dragon? No Fae would ever dare such a thing."

Isran shrugged. "It's the seduction of the black magic, Aimery. You're powerless now, unable to do more than make yourself hoarse as you scream for your lover. Even if I granted your magic back to you, you couldn't break the chains about your wrists."

"I will free Kyndra." The room spun, his mind screaming for his magic. He had to have it. It was the only way to save

Kyndra.

"I can give you the means to free her," Isran whispered in his ear.

Aimery jerked away from him. "I despise you."

"For now you do. I give it another day or two before you'll be begging me."

"Begging you for what?"

"Magic, Aimery. What else?"

Aimery threw back his head and laughed. He was walking a line of madness, the slightest tip and his mind would be gone forever. "You won't give me anything."

"That's right." Isran tapped his finger on his chin. "You're fighting your insanity. That's good. You need to keep fighting it."

"Let me see Kyndra," he bellowed and yanked on the chain.

Isran lifted his brows. "I told you, she's resting."

"Bring her here, Isran. I need to see her."

"No warrior such as yourself should have such a weakness, Aimery."

He hung his head, the frustration and despair sapping his energy. The manacles cut into his skin, sending rivets of blood down his arm, but he didn't care. His throat felt as though a dragon had scratched it, but he didn't care. He was going daft, but he didn't care. Nothing mattered without Kyndra.

Gods, how he missed her smile, the way her eyes crinkled at the corners when she got excited. He missed her smell, the feel of her hair in his fingers. He missed her strength, her passion.

He missed her.

Kyndra.

He didn't believe Isran. Kyndra had left the chamber bound and gagged. Anything could have happened to her. She could be dead now for all he knew. If Isran was lying, Aimery was going to track down the men who took her and kill them painfully and slowly.

Isran was talking, but he no longer cared what he had to say. He was a murderer, a thief—a liar. No one had ever deceived Aimery so, and it hurt. Isran had been like a brother to him. Aimery had shown him things, taught him things, he had never done before.

And this was how Isran repaid him.

It was only after the door closed behind Isran that Aimery lifted his head and continued calling for Kyndra. He couldn't give up hope that she was still alive.

Kyndra opened her eyes and blinked against the candle that flared next to the bed. She tentatively touched her cheek and, when there was no pain, she moved her jaw.

"You're healed."

Her gaze swung to the other side of the bed where Isran stood. "You healed me?"

"The pain was too much for you."

"Thank you."

"Don't thank me yet," he cautioned.

She sat up and noticed that she was clad in a plain cotton gown. "Where am I?"

"You're still in the castle." He walked to the foot of the bed and leaned his hands on the footboard. "You've been asleep a full day."

Kyndra noticed the lines of worry on his forehead, the way his lips pressed tightly together and his clenched hands. "What has happened? Is it Aimery? Is he all right?"

"Nay, he's not all right."

She threw aside the covers and knelt before him. "What has happened to him?"

Isran sighed and ran a hand down his face. "It's his mind. I fear it's gone. "

"Take me to him. Now." She jumped from the bed and walked to the door.

He put a hand on her arm to stop her. "Get dressed," he said and nodded with his head to the chair. "I'll wait outside."

Kyndra jerked off the gown before he had closed the door behind him. She hurried put on the cream gown she had worn the night before. The feel of the soft material made her think of Aimery. She yanked open the door to find Isran waiting for her.

"Why didn't you use your magic on Aimery?" she demanded as they started walking down the corridor.

Isran shrugged. "Who says I didn't."

"Did you?"

He glanced at her. "I told you I didn't want to kill Aimery."

That didn't mean he had to save him either. Dread pooled in her belly as she lifted her skirts so she could walk faster. They had just ascended a set of stairs when she heard her name. Her steps faltered, then slowed as she realized it was Aimery shouting for her.

Her gaze moved to Isran. "How long has he been doing this?"

"Since I took you."

Kyndra grabbed her skirts and ran down the hall to Aimery's chamber. She threw open the door to find him chained to the wall, blood caked on his wrists and arms, his head hanging between his shoulders as he continued to bellow her name.

"Aimery."

"He won't hear you," Isran said as he came up behind her. "His mind is gone."

She shook her head. "Nay. He's too strong."

Kyndra walked to Aimery and lifted his head in her hands. His eyes were shut, his face haggard. "Aimery. Open your eyes."

"Kyndra!"

Her heart ached to see him thus. It was as if he couldn't hear her, or refused to. "Aimery, please!"

When he still wouldn't open his eyes, she slapped his face, hoping to shock him enough that he would look at her. He didn't even flinch.

"I told you. His mind is gone."

"You shouldn't have let this happen," she whispered. Tears fell down her cheeks as she stared at the warrior who had vowed to protect her, the man who had showed her what it was like to be loved.

Isran turned her away from him.

Nothing made sense to her anymore. Why would Isran not kill them? Aimery was a threat, a warrior not to be taken lightly. Yet Isran said he didn't want to kill him. Then why keep him alive? Just because he admired him? That didn't make much sense to her.

Nay, Isran had to have something else planned.

"You said you were keeping me alive to help Aimery. You knew this would happen."

Isran smiled. "It's amazing what you can learn from black magic."

"So you think you can predict the future?"

"Nay. I can see into it, however."

"Are you sure you aren't seeing what you want to see?"

He laughed. "Ah, Kyndra. Now I see what attracted Aimery to you. You have a strength of spirit that fairly glows within you. Would you like me to tell you what your fellow priestesses think of your betrayal to their vows?"

Kyndra winced, unable to stop the hurt his words caused. "I knew what I was doing."

"Nay, you didn't. It was the magic that drew you in."

This time she laughed. "Is that what you think? I hate to disappoint you, but I had already decided to give in to my desire for Aimery before we entered the castle. Your magical music only set the mood."

"You lie."

The way he held himself still told her he hadn't liked what he heard. "I'm not. If your black magic is so powerful, why not find out for yourself."

Every time Aimery hollered for her she wanted to cry. His

voice was hoarse, barely discernable from the deep timbre she had come to love. He refused to stop, though she knew he must be in pain.

"Let me stay with him," she begged.

"Nay."

"Isran, you need me. Let me stay with him."

Isran looked from her to Aimery before he gave a brief nod and left the chamber. She heard the telltale click as he locked the door. She almost laughed. Where would she be going? She wasn't leaving the castle without Aimery, and he was in no condition to go anywhere.

She walked to him and brushed his hair away from his face. "You promised not to leave me. Come back to me, Aimery. I need you."

Chapter Sixteen

"I need you."

The words echoed in Aimery's head. He thought he caught the scent of Kyndra, but it was most likely another of Isran's tricks. How many times had Isran brought in a vision of Kyndra? How many times Aimery thought it was her, only to hear Isran's evil laugh? It was so many that Aimery no longer trusted his eyes.

He had stopped responding, shutting his eyes and his heart to the beseeching voices that sounded so similar to Kyndra's. But none of them were her. They might look like her, sound like her, but they didn't smell like her.

The more powerless he felt, the deeper into his insanity he sunk. He knew and could do nothing about it. He wasn't sure of Isran's game. Maybe the bastard just wanted to see how much he could make him suffer.

Aimery almost laughed at the thought. He had endured months of torture at Lugus' hand when he tried to take over the Fae realm, and not once had Aimery faltered. Yet now, the thought of Kyndra wounded or dying made him ready to give Isran whatever he wanted in return for her freedom.

And that's when it hit Aimery. Isran wanted something

from him. He wanted Aimery to break, to beg for Kyndra's life. That's when the son of a bitch would tell Aimery what he wanted.

The question was, how long could Aimery hold out. Already his mind was slipping through his fingers, breaking into tiny fragments that teased him with bouts of lucidity. Just as it did now.

For a moment, he could have staked his life that he smelled jasmine and sunshine. For just a heartbeat, he had dared to open his eyes in the hopes of seeing Kyndra.

And just as soon as it had come, it disappeared.

The illusion Isran had sent to him continued to speak, her soft voice speaking his name, begging him to open his eyes. But Aimery was no fool. He would not succumb to Isran's baiting. He would hold out. He would keep his mind together. Even if it shredded every last ounce of his being, he would fight for Kyndra.

He fisted his hands, no longer feeling the blood that had coated his arms. His arms were numb, his shoulders aching with every breath he took. Try as he might, his legs refused to hold him any longer. The more he tried, the more pain he brought onto the rest of his body. So, he hung there, his arms pulled out to his side, his knees nearly touching the floor. Pain was the only friend he had, for the pain reminded him why he was in Thav in the first place.

Aimery turned his wrist, letting the metal cut into his skin. He hissed in a breath when pain lanced through his shoulder.

"By all that's magical, what are you doing, you fool?"

He ignored the false Kyndra and focused on the pain of his body. Breath by agonizing breath he dove into the pain, pulling his mind back to him while he forced himself not to think of his magic.

Soft, cool hands touched his face and threaded through his hair. For just a moment, he let himself believe it was Kyndra, that she had come to him. But that's all he allowed himself, that one, brief moment in time. He didn't turn away from her, because that would only let her know he wasn't completely insane, and she would renew her efforts. Aimery wasn't strong enough to resist her, even knowing she wasn't the real Kyndra.

Even now he could feel her soft skin beneath his hands, hear her moans of pleasure as he thrust inside her. By the gods, she had been incredible, more than he had ever dreamed of.

"Kyndra!"

Kyndra jumped as Aimery shouted her name. She winced and tried to get him to drink the water once more. He never jerked away from her, but he didn't accept her either. It was almost as if he didn't know she was there.

For a few moments he had stopped his yelling, and she had thought it was because of her. Now she realized he had just sunk into insanity. Tears burned her eyes and fell onto her cheek. She dashed them away, hating her weakness and her inability to help him.

Now that she had seen him, she needed to pull herself together and figure out how she was going to free him, kill Isran, and get the egg back to the Fae realm. It was a daunting task, but one Aimery would have taken on in a heartbeat. It was the least she could do for him.

Kyndra set the goblet of water on the table and walked around the room. She hadn't paid much attention to it the previous night since all she had cared about was Aimery but now she let her gaze wander over it, looking for a way out.

She walked to the window and threw it open. Wind buffeted her face and made her gasp for breath. She shielded her eyes with her arm and leaned out of the window. That's when she saw the sheer drop down the jagged mountain. Even if she and Aimery survived the fall, they had nowhere to go. Isran and his guards would be on them in an instant.

Kyndra closed the window and leaned back against it. She rubbed her hands up and down her arms in a vain attempt to find warmth. Hopelessness settled into her stomach, and no matter how hard she tried, she couldn't push it away.

"Oh, Aimery," she whispered and ran her hand down the

bed.

She looked at the massive four poster bed, the dark wood etched with runes of some ancient civilization. The table and chairs and even the wood around the windows had the same runes. Kyndra walked to the door and found even more of the markings. She moved her fingers over the runes, wondering what they meant.

With a sigh she turned her back to the door and slid to the floor. Her gaze found Aimery, his voice barely discernable as he continued to scream her name. It was heart wrenching to see him struggle so, made even worse since she couldn't help him.

She drummed her fingers on her arm. She missed having the dragon wrapped around her arm, its flashing sapphire eyes reminding her of the blue dragons. Aimery had slid it off her arm the night before where it dropped on the floor.

Kyndra jerked away from the door and crawled to the bed when she remembered how Aimery had kicked it beneath the bed so Isran wouldn't notice it. Her hand closed over the cool metal and pulled it out from under the bed.

The dragon band was a sign of her warrior ability. All Fae knew what it meant for a woman to wear one. Aimery had been protecting her, giving her a chance to find a way to surprise Isran with her skills. She put the dragon on her arm, its head pointed toward her as its blue eyes winked at her through the candlelight.

She rose to her feet and walked to Aimery. By his furrowed brow and pinched lips he was in pain. If only she could heal him. She dipped her fingers into the goblet and ran them over his lips, wetting them.

"Come back to me, Aimery."

Once more he had stopped bellowing her name, and she used the time to wet his lips. He shifted his arm, and blood welled from a wound on his wrist to roll down his arm.

"What are you doing?" she asked and wiped away the blood.

She put her finger between his wrist and the manacles and felt the rusted metal. She winced when the metal cut into her skin. Kyndra jerked her finger out and started to wipe away the blood when it healed.

She blinked. With her heart pounding in her chest, she cut her finger again, deeper this time, and just as before, it healed.

"This cannot be."

Isran had taken her magic. He had told her he was the one to heal her, but had he spoken the truth? Had he returned her magic instead? If so, why?

Her head began to pound as she tried to understand what had happened. With everything going on with Aimery, she hadn't had time to wonder why she hadn't begun to go daft. Now she knew. Isran had given her back her magic.

Kyndra put her hands on either side of Aimery's face and tilted his head until she could see all of him. "Aimery, please. It's me, Kyndra. Open your eyes. Aimery, open your eyes."

He did nothing to give her any sign that he had heard her. Kyndra had never felt so alone in all her life. She was no match for Isran magically. She wrapped her arms around his neck and buried her face in his neck.

"I can't fight him. I need you."

After a deep breath, she lowered her arms and took a step away from him. The first thing she had to do was get him out of the chains. There had to be something Isran wanted, and she would discover what it was.

The door to Aimery's chamber opened. Isran leaned against the doorjamb, his arms crossed over his chest and a triumphant smile on his face. "Have you figured it all out yet?"

"When did you return my magic?"

"After I carried you to your new chamber."

She nodded, hating him anew. She had begun to think him misunderstood but, then again, that had been his intention. He liked keeping her guessing. It was nothing but a game to him, but she could also play games.

Kyndra faced him. "What do you want?"

"Power. I can never have enough." His gaze narrowed, and he pushed off the door. "What do you have on your arm?"

She smiled and turned her arm to look at the dragon cuff. "This? It's mine."

"You're a warrior?"

"Oh, aye, Isran. A warrior priestess, leader of the Blue Order."

He threw back his head and laughed. "Perfect!"

She had thought to give him pause with her title, but a sickening feeling fell into the pit of her stomach. "What is perfect?"

"You," he said and walked around her. He leaned close to her ear and whispered, "You are the answer to all my plans."

She opened her mouth to ask him what those plans were when he took her by the elbow and dragged her out of the room. Kyndra glanced over her shoulder to see Aimery's eyes open. And looking at her.

Chapter Seventeen

Aimery shook his head to clear his mind. He must be hallucinating again. It was the smell of jasmine and sunshine that had pulled him out of his madness, given him time to inflict more pain on himself.

Kyndra's whispered words had stilled his heart, because he had known instantly it was really her. He had tried to talk to her, to whisper her name, but his voice no longer worked. Each swallow was like needles going down his throat.

And then Isran had come into the room.

Aimery had tried to listen to them, but their voices were muffled, as if in a tunnel. When he was finally able to open his eyes, it was to see Isran leading Kyndra out of the chamber. The only thing that let Aimery know he hadn't imagined her scent was the dragon on her arm.

None of the illusions Isran had put before him had worn it, which meant it really had been Kyndra with him. If only he had realized it sooner, he could have talked to her, touched her.

He yanked on the chains, yearning for his magic like never before.

His mind whirled, jerking him down into a pit that threatened to never let him out. Aimery fought against the lunacy, daring himself to believe in Kyndra, to hope.

"Kyndra," he whispered. "You're not alone."

But it was too late. She was gone from him once again.

Hope sprung in Kyndra's chest. Aimery had opened his eyes, he had seen her. Maybe somehow she had reached him. She didn't know how but, if she could get back to him, maybe she could talk to him. Together, she had no doubt they could figure out a plan to stop Isran.

Isran's fingers dug into her arm. She refused to let him know he had hurt her. When he wasn't able to get a response that way, he quickened his steps, causing her to trip over her skirts and fall to her knees.

He yanked her up, his lips pulled back in a sneer. "Your thoughts betray you, priestess."

A shiver of apprehension raced down her spine. "I've blocked you."

"Did you not believe me or Aimery when we told you black magic was stronger than Fae magic? You can put up all the measly defenses you have, and yet I'll be able to break through every one of them."

"So you know I want you destroyed. You've known that from the beginning. Why get upset over it now?"

He gave her a jerk. "Upset? I'm not upset."

"Really?" She noted the tick at the corner of his left eye.

"Oh, I'm not at all happy that you were able to break through to Aimery but, in the end, I think it will be to my benefit."

Kyndra wrenched herself out of his grasp. "What are you talking about?"

"While you've been...healing...I've been playing mind games with Aimery. Again and again I put an illusion of you in his chamber. It was quite funny the first ten times to see him try to talk to the illusion, to touch her."

Kyndra swallowed, the bile rising in her throat. "All the

goodness that made you a Fae is completely gone, isn't it?"

"Every last drop, priestess."

She steeled herself and fisted her hands at her side. "What do I have to do to get you to release Aimery?"

"There's just one thing I want from you." He took a step toward her and touched her cheek.

Kyndra had to fight to keep from jerking away, but she would do whatever he wanted for Aimery. "What is that?"

"Perform the ceremony."

"The ceremony? What ceremony?"

He dropped his hand, his gaze narrowed in laughter. "As a priestess of the Order, a leader of the Blue Order, you don't know?"

"Apparently not."

"Now that is amusing. What was Julieth thinking in not informing at least you of the consequences should I take over Thav?"

Kyndra shook her head. "You don't know what you're talking about."

"Oh, but I do. You see, my sweet, not only do I bathe in the yolk of the egg, but I need a priestess of the Order to infusion the dragon with me."

Her heart slammed into her rib cage, threatening to burst from her chest. "You must be jesting. Julieth would have told me. In any event, she would never have dared to send me."

"But she did. Why is that?"

"You must have it wrong. There doesn't need to be a ceremony. I'm not needed." She didn't know why she gave him the power of that knowledge, but his words had confused her, frightened her. It put into question everything Julieth had ever told her, and that wasn't good.

Isran shrugged. "Believe what you want, but I'm right. You want to save Aimery from his madness, then join me."

Kyndra looked at the hand he held out for her. What he asked went against everything she had lived for, everything she had come to fight against. She loved the dragons, but her love for Aimery was more.

A tear spilled down her cheek as she realized she had fallen in love with the Commander. And she would never get the chance to tell him.

"I'll do it, but you have to return Aimery to our realm."

"I can't do that."

"Then I cannot help you." Kyndra was determined to see him safe. She didn't like bargaining with his life, but it was a gamble she had to take. For as long as Isran was willing.

Isran beckoned to her with his fingers. "Come, come, priestess. You don't want Aimery to suffer more do you?"

A strangled bellow of pain came from Aimery's room.

"I will release him from his bonds, but Aimery stays in Thav," Isran said. "It's my final offer."

"You need me. You will be willing to forgo your ceremony without me?"

"I'll have you one way or another, priestess. Take what I'm offering before I change my mind."

Kyndra looked at his hand and knew in her heart this was her last chance for Aimery. She put her hand in Isran's. "Release Aimery. I'll perform your ceremony."

The smile on Isran's face made her blood run cold.

"Come. There is much to prepare."

Kyndra glanced at Aimery's chamber. "Can I see him? To make sure you've released him?"

"I keep my promises," he said and pulled her after him. "You can see him later. That I vow."

She had no choice but to go with Isran, even though every fiber of her being told her to go to Aimery. She wanted to see him once more before he realized what she had become, before he sensed the black magic within her. Kyndra had known taking Isran's deal would seal her fate, but she had done it anyway. Maybe once she learned how to control the black magic she could attack him and end it all.

They descended several flights of stairs and traversed a maze of corridors before they reached a set of double doors at the end of a hallway. Isran pushed them open and motioned her inside.

Kyndra wasn't surprised at the opulent surrounds of the chamber. It was rectangle with an arched ceiling. A rug of deep crimson ran down the middle of the chamber to the gilded throne that set on a raised landing.

Large candelabras of gold hung from the walls, and guards stood along the chamber, long spears in their hands. Movement in a corner caught her eye as she and Isran walked to his throne. That's when she saw what looked like a large birdcage, and inside was a man, his dark eyes solemn as he gazed at her.

"Priestess, let me introduce Eldar, the previous ruler of Thav."

A lump of sympathy formed in her chest at the haggard appearance of the old man, bent with age. His face was wrinkled, and his shoulder length hair was snow white. He gripped the bars of the cage, and Kyndra noted that his hands didn't shake.

"That's what being in control of Thav without the benefit of a dragon's egg will do to you," Isran whispered in her ear. "He looks frail, but he isn't. His mind is sharper than ever."

"Then how did you get control?"

Isran laughed. "Men are easily swayed with the promise of power and coin. Eldar thought his men loyal to him. He was wrong."

"Will you make that same mistake?"

"I'm not that foolish. In my position, you can trust no one."

She snorted. "Yet, you are trusting me to perform the ceremony."

He turned her to face him, his fingers biting into her shoulders. "Don't even think of trying something, priestess. I will kill you in a blink."

She took his threat seriously and nodded so he would release her. Kyndra took a deep breath when Isran walked to the throne and lowered himself in the huge chair. He beckoned her forward and, though she didn't want to be near him, she lifted her skirt and climbed the steps.

"I knew you would look lovely in that gown," Isran said. "I have no doubt once you get your first taste of black magic, you will understand why it's so seductive. The power, the energy that courses through you." He took in a deep breath. "There's nothing like it."

"You are sure of what it will do to me."

He laughed. "My dear priestess, no one can withstand it. No one."

"What will you do to me once I finish the ceremony?"

His finger caressed up her arm. "I have plans for you, plans that you will, no doubt, enjoy as much as I do."

The thought of him touching her body, caressing her, kissing her as Aimery had done left her sick to her stomach. But she couldn't worry about that now. There was so much more to think about.

"Where is the egg?"

Isran smiled. "In due time. First, we must begin your lessons."

"Lessons?"

"What Julieth didn't tell you is that if a priestess of the Order turns to black magic, she will have the power to bind the dragon to someone. The binding will increase my power a hundredfold. I won't just be invincible, priestess, I will be inexorable."

Kyndra's knees threatened to buckle. "Why wouldn't she tell me? Never before has that been spoken in the Order."

"There is much about black magic that isn't spoken about in the Fae realms."

"Then how do you know of it?"

He chuckled. "It isn't just power I gain with the use of my magic, priestess. It's knowledge. Secrets long held about black magic, its source, its power, its strengths are given to the users. Soon, you will understand what I mean."

Kyndra was angry that Julieth hadn't told her of the

ceremony. She understood why it wasn't taught in the Order but, knowing what they were up against, Julieth could have told her before they arrived on Thav.

Did Aimery know?

She liked to think he didn't, but what frightened her more than anything was the little thrill that shot through her at the knowledge that she would gain strength in her magic. She told herself it was to fight Isran, but she wasn't sure how true that was.

"Ready?"

Kyndra turned her gaze to his. "Nay."

"Don't fight it. I see the excitement in your eyes, the yearning to learn if black magic is as luring as everyone says."

"You're misreading my hatred for you for excitement."

Isran threw back his head and laughed. "The more I'm around you the more I realize what captivated Aimery so."

The mention of Aimery sent a stab of longing through her heart.

Isran rose so that she faced the doors they had entered. His mouth moved to her ear as he stood behind her. "To use black magic is very simple, priestess."

As he spoke two guards walked into the chamber dragging a young boy. They threw the boy down, his torn and bloodied tunic falling off his shoulders as he turned to face them.

"He's a thief," Isran whispered.

"What did he steal?"

"A loaf of bread. The price for thievery is death."

Kyndra tried to ignore the boy's gaunt frame, the welts and bruises staining his fair skin. He was starving, yet he stood with his shoulders back and his head high as he waited for the guards to attack.

On her realm, no one killed. To kill was to use black magic. If there was a crime, the criminal went before a judge and jury and learned his sentence. Murder was not tolerated on the Realm of the Fae.

Despite that, Kyndra couldn't allow the boy to be killed

because he lacked the coin to buy food. She fisted her hands and tried to look away as the guards pulled their swords from their scabbards, the sound echoing in the chamber.

To give the boy credit, he didn't flinch or beg for his life. He had known the consequences for his actions, and he had taken a chance. But he was just a child, a starving child.

Isran moved her hair so his lips could graze her ears. "What will you do?"

Kyndra fisted her hands. The laws of Thav were in place for a reason. Who was she to challenge them?

He's just a boy!

Her gaze was locked on the guards. Their weapons pulled back, ready to strike.

Time slowed as she watched the blades plunging toward the boy's small chest. What kind of Fae would she be to let a child die for trying to give himself nourishment? Her eyes closed. She gave in to the need to save the child.

A surge of power rushed through her, startling her with its ferocity, its allure. Her eyes flew open and lips parted as she gasped. Just as her knees gave out, Isran's arms wrapped around her.

"See how easy that was, priestess," he murmured in her ear. "You can feel the magic pulsing through you, strengthening your power the same time you're gaining knowledge."

The chamber spun around her. She had merely saved the boy's life. How could that have taken her toward black magic? Her gaze found the boy who stood over the two guards lying motionless on the floor.

"You killed them. For the boy."

Kyndra shook her head at Isran's words. She hadn't meant to kill them, just protect the defenseless boy. "Nay."

"Don't fight it," Isran urged. He turned her so that he lifted her in his arms. "There's no turning back now, priestess."

Chapter Eighteen

Aimery rolled onto his back and groaned at the aches pounding through his body. Sunlight filtered through the window. How many days he had slept, he wasn't sure. He pushed the sheet from his body, noting that he was still naked. His nose itched, but he was afraid to lift his hand for fear it wouldn't work after hanging so long in the chains.

But the itch wouldn't be ignored. His finger found the tip of his nose and scratched without too much pain. A heartbeat later he realized he was in his bed. All thoughts of pain fled as he jerked upright in search of Kyndra. One glance around his chamber confirmed he was alone.

Aimery ran a hand down his face. Where had Isran taken Kyndra now, and what was the bastard up to that he would release him? Isran was cunning. He liked to tease and torment, gaining a gleeful, sickening pleasure out of it.

The need to feel his magic threatened to take him back down into the pit of madness, but he fought it. He would be no good to Kyndra insane.

It was the smell of food that drew him from the bed. He didn't bother to look for clothes as he stumbled his way to the table. His hands shook from lack of use and weakness. He spilled more wine than he got into the goblet as he poured. It took two tries before he was able to pull meat off the bone. Aimery didn't know what it was, nor did he care. He needed food and quickly.

The first bite was like a taste of bliss. His mouth watered for more, his stomach growling as he ate. Aimery finished off the slab of meat and the entire loaf of bread. Then he delved into the delicious pastries arranged so neatly on the golden platter. Only then did he allow himself to finish the jug of wine.

With his stomach full and his strength returning, Aimery found himself thinking if Isran and what his next step would be. He hadn't killed Kyndra or him. But why? What use did either one of them serve Isran? Aimery wouldn't stop until Isran was dead. Surely Isran had to realize that.

There was a soft knock at his door. Aimery's head jerked to the door, his heart quickening as he wondered if it was Kyndra. As the door swung open and a servant stepped into the chamber with her head bowed, Aimery sat back and sighed.

He was such a fool. Isran wouldn't allow Kyndra to walk around the castle, and he most certainly wouldn't let her come to him.

"Yer bath, milord," the servant said.

Aimery watched while the tub was brought in and filled with water. The tendrils of heat rising from the tub beckoned him to relax his aching body in the heat. He didn't wait for the servants to leave as he rose and walked to the tub. The female glanced at him beneath her lowered lashes, a blush staining her cheek.

He lowered himself in the tub and groaned. The water felt wonderful. He leaned his head back and closed his eyes. For whatever reason, Isran was allowing him to build his strength, and Aimery was going to take every chance he got to do just that.

"Do ye...need...anythin' else, milord?"

Aimery cracked open an eye to find the servant girl

standing beside the tub. So, Isran had sent her to tempt him. "Nay. You may leave."

She licked her lips and opened her mouth as if she would say more, but she turned on her heel and left.

The chamber once more his, Aimery relaxed in the tub until the water began to cool. Only then did he bathe. After he dried off, he wrapped the towel around his waist. As he walked to the table for more wine he noticed the black tunic and breeches laid out for him. He didn't wish to walk around naked, so he put on the clothes.

Once his boots were on, he looked beneath the bed for his weapons and found them gone as was the missive from Theron. Isran had wasted little time in seizing everything Aimery had. All he had to do now was wait for he knew Isran would return very, very soon.

Kyndra stared at herself in the mirror. She looked the same, but inside she was different. She had felt it since that moment in Isran's throne room.

Black Magic.

She had taken a life. Regardless of why she had done it, she had done it. And in doing so had committed herself down a path where there was no return. A path that had ensured she would never see her realm again, never see the beauty of the dragons flying the sky or hear their call.

Never look into Aimery's eyes and see his desire for her.

A tear slipped down her cheek. Kyndra hastily wiped it away. She hadn't had a choice in the matter. Not only could she not let the boy die, but she couldn't let anything happen to Aimery. He was much stronger than her. He would be able to end Isran's rule and save the egg.

How she longed to touch him again, just once more wrap her arms around him and feel his warmth. Her sex throbbed, and moisture gathered between her thighs as she thought about his rod sliding into her, thrusting hard and fast.

Her breasts ached for his touch. She cupped her breasts and sucked in a breath when her fingers grazed her sensitive nipples. Her body heated, yearning for Aimery's caress, to feel his lips on her, wringing cries of pleasure from her.

The black magic was still new in her, and Aimery didn't have his magic. There was a chance he wouldn't realize what she had become. The kernel of hope had formed in her heart and wouldn't be ignored. Kyndra rose from the stool and left her chamber. No one stopped her as she walked through the castle to Aimery's room.

The closer she got, the more her body yearned for his touch. When she came to his chamber, she stopped and placed her hand on the door. Isran had assured her Aimery had been released and seen to, but she didn't know if she could believe him.

After seeing Aimery lost in his madness, she wasn't sure what she would find if she opened the door. But she had to see him.

She opened the door and looked inside. The bed was mused, the sheet puddle on the floor. Water pooled near the tub and a towel had been tossed onto the bed. Isran hadn't lied. She was surprised by that, and also relieved.

"Kyndra?"

Her head swiveled around to the table to find Aimery. He looked hail except for the dark circles beneath his eyes and the lines of worry on his brow. "Aye. It's me."

"What are you doing here?" He narrowed his gaze as he rose, as if he didn't trust her.

If only he knew. "I've been allowed to see you."

"Why?"

She swallowed and shrugged. "I don't know. Who knows why Isran does what he does."

He seemed to accept her answer.

Kyndra closed the door behind her and walked to Aimery. She reached up and ran her hand down his face. "Are you in much pain?"

"It's tolerable."

"And your mind? Are you with me?"

He lifted one shoulder in a shrug. "For now. It gets more difficult with each hour."

"You can withstand it," she said and forced a smile. "If anyone can, it's you."

His hands grasped her shoulders and pulled her closer. "What happened to you? Isran told me you had been hurt?"

"It…was nothing." She didn't want to tell him how terrified she had been of being raped, of the pain she had experienced at the men's hands.

"It was something."

"Believe it or not, Isran saved me."

Aimery snorted. "The one thing I've learned about Isran is that he doesn't do anything for free."

"I agree."

"You won't tell me what happened?"

She swallowed. "I was spared, Aimery. Leave it at that."

"But you were injured."

"Only a little."

"How?"

He wouldn't leave it alone, she realized. She would have to tell him part of it, but no more. "One of the guards hit me."

Aimery's brow furrowed. "He struck you? I'll kill him."

"No need. Isran already did it."

That only seemed to anger Aimery more. "Be careful around him. He uses people's weaknesses against them."

Dread pooled in her belly. Isran had said as much to her, gloating that he had finally found Aimery's weakness. "Do you have a weakness?"

"Aye, and Isran knows it's you. I know he'll use you against me. I just haven't figured out how yet."

Kyndra had a feeling turning her to black magic was part of Isran's grand scheme.

"Just like I don't know why he's kept us alive."

She knew the answer to that. "Isran says that he admires

you, that you are one of the greatest warriors the Fae has ever seen. He said he couldn't kill you because there would never be another like you again."

"That's shite, and you know it."

She wasn't so sure. Aimery was different from the other Fae. He had accomplished much more with the humans than any Fae ever before. But it wasn't just what he had done on Earth, it was what he had done for other realms, including their own. It was no wonder Isran couldn't kill him. How could anyone kill something as magnificent as Aimery?

"Kyndra?"

She threw her arms around him, needing his strength. His enfolded her in his embrace.

"You're shaking. What's wrong?"

She couldn't tell him the truth, so she settled for something close to it. "Isran has returned my powers."

"Good. Use them to get the egg."

"I can't. His power is too great."

Aimery set her away from him and cupped her face in his hands. "Kyndra, do whatever he asks. Just stay alive long enough for me to figure a way to end this."

Their gazes locked, and desire flared between them. Isran and his threat were forgotten as they lost themselves in each other. Kyndra's lids closed as Aimery lowered his head and took her mouth in a soft, coaxing kiss.

Her body melted against him, eager to taste more of him. The kiss quickly turned fierce, the desire between them too great. Her sex throbbed when she felt his thick cock pressed against her.

"By the gods, how I hunger for you," he murmured between kisses.

She clawed at his tunic, needing to feel his skin under her hands. With one jerk he pulled it over his head and yanked her back against him.

"I thought I had lost you."

Her tears made him blur. "I'll always be yours. Always."

"Kyndra."

He said her name as if it were a prayer, spoken softly, lovingly. The tears she had tried to hold at bay spilled onto her cheeks.

"Why do you cry?"

"Because I've finally found you. Because I'd give up everything to be with you. Because I fear what the future holds."

He brushed her tears away. "I will find a way to free us."

She was grateful when he kissed her again. If they had continued talking, she was liable to confess what she had become, and the thought of Aimery's beautiful eyes filled with loathing was more than she could take.

His kiss stole her breath and heated her blood. He kissed as if their very lives depended upon it, as if it were the last chance they would be together. And for Kyndra, it most likely was. She put all her love, her hope, in the kiss. She didn't have the courage to tell him of her love, but she could show him.

She helped him take off her gown then eagerly aided him in the removal of his boots and breeches. When they were both naked, they stood bathed in the sunlight.

"I'll never get enough of you."

She smiled and ran her thumb over his lips. "Good, because I want more of you."

"You can have me for as long as you want."

She was swept into his arms as he kissed down her neck, nipping her skin with his lips and tongue. Kyndra forgot about Isran, the black magic and the egg. She forgot about her vows to the Order, the Blue dragons and their realm. She forgot everything but Aimery and his wonderful hands caressing her body.

His hands were everywhere, stroking her, learning her. The force of her desire made her tremble and her sex clench greedily for his touch. Aimery's hand cupped the back of her head as he leaned her over his arm and kissed down her shoulder and across to her breast.

The first touch of his mouth on her nipple brought a sigh past her lips. His tongue circled the tiny bud, teasing it until it was hard and aching. Only then did he draw her nipple into his mouth and suckle. Kyndra moaned and clutched his head, holding him against her.

His other hand kneaded her bottom, grinding her against his hard cock. Kyndra lifted her leg to wrap around his waist. She wanted him inside her, to feel him stretch and fill her. Moisture gathered between her legs. His rod rubbed against her pearl sending ripples of pleasure over her.

"You taste delectable," he murmured against her skin.

He lifted her and placed her on the bed, but when he covered her with his body Kyndra pushed at his shoulders. She rolled him until he was on his back. Then she straddled his hips and ran her hands over his chest.

She rose up on her knees and took his rod in her hand. Her lips parted when she spotted the bead of fluid at the tip of his cock. She used her finger to smear the liquid around his head before she lowered herself on him.

His fingers gripped her hips as she slowly sank down his thick rod.

Only when she was fully seated did she begin to rotate her hips. She started out slow but, at the pleasure and desire washing over Aimery's face, she quickened her tempo. When she rose up and down his length, he moaned her name, his gaze glued between their bodies.

"I can't last," Aimery ground out.

Kyndra's climax was already building. She could feel the tension mounting, her body tightening just before she peaked. "Then come with me."

Aimery reached up and pinched her nipples, sending her over the edge. Her breath locked in her lungs as her orgasm exploded. She could feel herself clenching around his rod, heard his moans as his cock jumped inside her, his seed filling her womb.

She drifted on the bliss of her climax for hours or days, she wasn't sure, but when she opened her eyes it was to find herself in Aimery's arms, his beautiful swirling blue eyes staring at her.

Chapter Nineteen

Aimery smoothed Kyndra's dark locks away from her face and kissed her forehead. Her passion, her fire stole his breath. He had refused to allow Isran to come between them as they made love. But now, in the afterglow, Aimery couldn't help but think of their predicament.

Kyndra's finger traced his eyebrow. "What are you thinking about?"

He turned so that he faced her, though his arm was still around her. "You."

"Liar."

He grinned. He didn't want to talk of Isran or the dragon's egg, not yet. Not until they had to. "What is it like in the Order?"

"Wonderful." She smiled, her gaze taking a wistful look. "I think it is much like your army. There are rules, of course. Your army takes an oath to serve our realm and their king and queen."

"Aye, but I don't make my men take vows of celibacy. Why do they ask that of you?"

"The dragons need to be our sole purpose. Long ago, when the Order first began, there were some who were married. The duties to their families took precedence to the dragons. So the High Priestess decided that to be a priestess in the Order, one must give everything to the Order."

Aimery ran his thumb over her lips, wanting to kiss her again. "Has anyone left the Order because they wanted a family?"

"A few. We go through rigorous training before we take our vows.

To be in the Order is not something to be taken lightly. Only a tenth of the girls who come to the Temple will become priestesses."

"And how many become warriors?"

She grinned and glanced at the dragon cuff on her arm. "Even fewer."

"Then you are truly unique. No High Priestess whom I have known about has also been a warrior."

"Nay. None ever has been."

"You were to be the first."

She shrugged. "Things change."

"Will you return to the Order once we get back?"

"Will you return to the palace?"

Aimery would give it all up, everything, just to be with her. He had found the one thing that could make him complete. He wasn't about to let her go. Not now. Not ever.

But now wasn't the time to make those kinds of confessions. First, he had to get them free of Thav, and to do that he had to kill Isran.

"Have you spoken to Isran?"

She nodded her head.

"Has he divulged anything?"

She licked her lips. "He is preparing to crack the egg."

"Did he say when?"

"In the next day or so. He also has Eldar locked in a cage in the throne room."

"Eldar? You mean Isran didn't kill him?"

"Nay. Eldar looks so old and frail that a strong wind could

break him in two. Yet, there is something in his eyes that tells me he is stronger than he appears."

Aimery considered her words. "Do you think you could get Eldar to side with us? If I could free him, together we could fight Isran."

"You don't understand just how powerful Isran has become. It's…frightening. Besides, you don't have your magic."

"Not yet, but I intended to get it back."

"How?"

Aimery smiled. "Isran is overconfident. He thinks his magic could defeat mine easily."

"Can it?"

"Maybe. Maybe not," he answered with a shrug. "I intend to make Isran think he doesn't need to fear me, that there is no reason not to give me my magic."

"Won't he get suspicious? Why would you want your magic back so desperately if you cannot use it against him?"

"To keep from going insane. Even now I'm fighting it, but it is easier with you in my arms."

Her lips turned up in a smile. "Do you think your plan could work? Isran has a way of learning everything."

That made Aimery pause. He had forgotten that little tidbit. "He returned your magic, yes?"

"Aye."

"Have you tried to block him from your mind?"

She nodded. "And failed miserably. He probably knows everything we're talking about now."

He could be, but not unless he was occupied elsewhere. Aimery had no way of knowing it. For all he knew, Isran had his full concentration on them, learning everything. "There has to be some way you can block him."

Her gaze lowered. "I will find a way."

There was something in her tone that told him there was something between her and Isran. He didn't think he could stand it if she had betrayed him and sided with Isran. Kyndra had been untouched before him, so he didn't think she could fake what was between them.

Still…

"Kyndra, what have you been doing?"

Her gaze met his. "Surviving."

"Good." He forced a smile, but he knew, deep in his gut, something was wrong. "We're in this together."

"If you think I'm with Isran, you're wrong."

Aimery took a deep breath. "I don't mean to make you feel that way, but I know how he is. He's manipulative. He'll do whatever he has to do and say whatever he has to say to get you to do what he wants. You know he uses people's weaknesses."

"I'm with you. Only you. Whatever I do, I will do it with the intention of fulfilling our mission."

The urgency in her gaze told him she needed him to believe her. "All right."

She sighed and snuggled against him. Aimery held her until her breathing evened into sleep. His fingers traced the dragon's head on her cuff. The sapphire eyes regarded him solemnly.

His weakness was Kyndra, but what was Isran using on her? It couldn't be the egg because Isran planned to use it. Could it be that Isran was using him? Did Kyndra care about him deeply enough that Isran was able to use it against her?

He was going to have to tell her not to trust Isran, especially when it came to him. If Isran had wanted him dead, he would already be dead. There was nothing Kyndra could do that would prevent that.

If only he still had his weapons.

Kyndra woke slowly, blinking several times. She was surprised to find night had fallen. The room was dark, but she knew she and Aimery weren't alone. She sat up and turned to find Isran sitting at the foot of the bead, leaning against one of the posters.

She glanced at Aimery to find him sleeping before she wrapped the blanket around herself. She rose from the bed and covered Aimery with another blanket.

"Aren't you going to talk to me?" Isran asked.

"Why? You know everything anyway."

"Do I?" He scratched his chin. "I probably do, but it only courteous to acknowledge me."

She turned to glare at him. "Is it courteous to watch two people make love? To listen to their thoughts?"

"Ah. You're angry."

"Angry doesn't begin to describe how I feel."

Isran chuckled and rose from the bed. "I gather you didn't tell Aimery that you've drifted to the dark side? I don't think our Commander would have taken it well at all."

"Stop," she said and ran her hand through her hair. "Just stop. I cannot take this. I'll do whatever you want but allow Aimery to return home."

"I can't."

Kyndra signed and picked up her gown.

"Aimery is an intelligent Fae. He knows that I'm using him against you, just as I'm using you against him. He's spent most of the past few hours trying to find a way to block me from his mind."

Her body still hummed from the delicious lovemaking. She wasn't ready to leave Aimery and face a future that didn't have him in it.

"You won't have long to wait now," Isran said and walked to the door. "At dusk, it begins."

Kyndra's knees buckled. She crumpled to the floor as Isran left the chamber. Her heart pounded so loudly in her chest she was sure it would wake Aimery. They had mere hours to gather a plan.

Yet she knew in her heart it was useless to hope. Isran was too powerful to deny. He would use the egg, he would become invincible. And she and Aimery were doomed to suffer whatever torment he decided upon them.

The only difference was, she wouldn't be able to come to Aimery as she did now. Once he realized what she had become, he would turn his back on her. And he had every right to do it. She had become the very thing she despised above all else.

She looked at Aimery sleeping so peacefully. She let go of the blanket and crawled to him. His hand hung over the side of the bed, and she laced her fingers with his. Just being near him gave her strength to face the next few hours.

Moments ticked by into hours. The first rays of sunlight made her sit up. She glanced at Aimery to find him still sleeping. She should have woken him, told him what was going to happen. But she had feared the knowledge would send him teetering over the edge. He needed to be as coherent as possible. If he knew she had turned to black magic, that there was nothing they could say that Isran didn't know, his madness would consume him.

She would rather see his hate because at least then he would be sane. And a sane Aimery would find a way. Of that she was positive.

Kyndra put on her gown. She had just finished combing her hair when the door to the chamber opened. Two guards stood waiting for her. She didn't have to be told what for. Isran had given her and Aimery all the time he would.

She pulled off her dragon cuff and laid it in Aimery's palm. It was her way of saying farewell and facing what was to come. No longer was she the head of the Blue Order, no longer was she a priestess.

She was Isran's to use as he pleased.

Kyndra followed the guards as they led her to her chamber to find a bath waiting for her. She wasn't surprised to find another gown for her, this one in crimson. Kyndra ran her hand over the soft, silky material.

"Do you like it?"

She turned her head to look at Isran over her shoulder. "Does it matter?"

"It does."

She wasn't fool enough to believe anything he said.

"I let you waste enough time with Aimery. I had thought you would thank me for that."

"Thank you," she murmured.

"I can smell him on you."

Kyndra smiled and turned away from him.

"Get cleaned up. You have work to do before tonight to strengthen your magic."

She didn't move until the door shut behind him. Though she knew it wouldn't hold him, she bolted the door and removed the gown. She hurried to wash. Isran was right, after all. She needed to gain strength.

After she had dried off, she pulled on the crimson gown. It slid sensuously down her body, reminding her of Aimery and the delicious way he made her blood heat with longing. She looked into the floor length mirror at herself.

The gown dipped in a low V in the front, showing an ample amount of her breasts. It clung to her waist before draping gently over her hips to fall at her feet. The matching crimson shoes were soft soled and hugged her feet.

It wasn't until she sat at her vanity to comb her hair that she saw the ruby necklace. She flung it aside and took a deep breath. She would wear the gowns because she refused to go naked in front of him, but it stopped there. No other "gift" from him would be accepted. And she hoped it made him angry. She wanted to rile him, to make him seethe as she did.

After she brushed her hair, she plaited two braids that began at her temples and met at the back of her head. The rest she left unadorned to hang freely about her. Aimery had loved to thread his fingers through her tresses.

She fisted her hands, feeling the black magic rise with her anger. She didn't try to hold it back as it infused her, consumed her. Isran had said it would be easy, and it was. So very easy to accept the power made every one of her senses stronger. She felt the power thrum through her, urging her to use more of it, to grow the magic.

With one last thought to Aimery and what could have been, she unleashed her power.

Chapter Twenty

Theron paced the vaulted foyer of Lugus' home. Ahryn's labor had been difficult, but that wasn't what had kept him away from his brother the past couple of nights. It was Aimery. Something had gone wrong, terribly wrong.

He glanced up when he heard a noise to find Lugus leaning against a doorway. His face was lined with fatigue, but he wore the silly grin of a new father. "I've never been so scared in my life."

"I know." Theron smiled despite the fears gripping him. "It was the same when Rufina had Nearra. I suspect it will be so again when our next child comes. Have you named your son yet?"

"Charon. After our father."

Theron nodded. Lugus had been accused of their father's murder, which had lead to his banishment from their realm. Had Lugus not garnered his powers, they would never have known that he hadn't killed their father, that he had died accidentally. Theron was still ashamed that he had so readily accused his own brother.

"Father would like that," he said.

Lugus shrugged. "I hope so. It was Ahryn's idea, but it

seems to fit the babe."

"Will Ahryn be all right?"

"No one expected her to have such a tough labor and, if not for our magic, I fear I would have lost her and Charon. But, aye, she will be fine. She's resting now." He pushed off the door and walked to Theron. "I'm sorry I had to leave Aimery and Kyndra."

"Don't," Theron said. "I would have done the same had Rufina called to me."

"Now that my son is born, I can return to Thav."

"I don't think that's a wise decision, brother."

Lugus frowned. "What has happened? Have you heard from them?"

"Nay, I have heard nothing, which leads me to believe our worst suspicions have come to light."

"Isran."

Theron nodded. "Aimery would have sent me a message letting me know he had reached Eldar and spoken with him."

"If something happened to Aimery, would Kyndra know to do the same?"

"I don't know." Theron ran his hand down his face. "I know Aimery would protect her with his very life if need be."

Lugus blew out a breath. "Let me go to them."

"I can't. Ahryn would never forgive me if I lost you to Isran as well."

"But you don't know if you've lost Aimery and Kyndra. We won't know that until I go."

"Nay, brother," Theron said. "Don't defy me in this."

"There can be only two reasons you haven't heard from Aimery. Either he's dead."

"Or Isran has taken over," Theron finished. "I know. I've been over this and over this for the last few days."

Lugus' gaze narrowed. "There's something else? What is it?"

"I was paid a visit by Julieth."

"The High Priestess? What did she want?"

"She didn't want anything. She wanted to impart a bit of knowledge that no one, not even Kyndra, knew about."

"This doesn't sound good."

Theron shook his head. "It isn't."

"Spit it out then. We can't do anything until we know what it is."

"Everyone knows that to steal a dragon's egg and bathe in the yolk after using black magic will make you invincible."

"Aye."

Theron hesitated. "What the Order has kept so secret that only the High Priestesses know is that if there is a priestess of the Order who can be convinced to perform a ceremony during the cracking of the egg then Isran's power will never be contained."

Lugus turned on his heel and walked to a table where he poured two goblets of wine. He handed one to Theron and drank deeply before he wiped his mouth and cursed.

"My thoughts exactly," Theron murmured.

Lugus tapped a finger on his leg. "If Julieth knew this, why did she send Kyndra? Why send a priestess at all?"

"I asked her the same question. She said the dragons told her to do it."

"Shite."

Theron drained the goblet and poured himself more wine. "My question is, do you think Isran could turn Kyndra to his side?"

"I don't know. I do know that Aimery would do everything he could to stop it."

"Would it be enough, though? No man has sway over the priestesses."

Lugus chuckled. "You didn't see how Aimery was looking at her then, did you?"

Theron paused as he lifted the goblet to his lips. "What?"

"Aimery was quite taken with the beautiful warrior priestess."

"And Kyndra?"

Lugus shrugged one shoulder. "She noticed him, if that's what you're asking. What happened after I left is anyone's guess."

"Despite Isran and Aimery's friendship, I know very little about Isran."

"There's not much to know. He was known for his tricks. He liked to manipulate people into doing what he wanted."

"In which case, he would manipulate Kyndra and Aimery."

Lugus nodded. "He needs the priestess and, if Kyndra is smart, she'll have kept Aimery alive as well."

"All this is assuming Isran has taken over."

"I think it's safe to say that has happened."

Theron sighed heavily. "Everything relies on Aimery and Kyndra."

"All we can do is ready the realm."

"I need you to command the army," Theron said. "I know you've just been blessed with your first child and your wife is still weak—"

"I'll do whatever you need," Lugus interrupted him. "Let me get Ahryn settled, and I'll be at the palace."

Theron nodded, grateful once again to have his brother back in the realm.

Aimery knew the instant he opened his eyes Kyndra was gone. He sat up and sighed, wishing she had woken him. It was only then that he felt something in his hand. As soon as he saw the dragon cuff, he knew Isran had managed to turn Kyndra to his side. He didn't know what Isran had planned for her but, whatever it was, it was bad enough that she had decided not to tell him.

He swallowed and focused on the image of her face in his mind instead of the pull of the madness. He would not succumb. He would not!

After several moments, he opened his eyes, his breathing ragged and his heart pounding in his ears as if he had run from one side of the realm to the other. So far he had managed to control the madness, but how much longer would that last? How long could he continue to fight it until he gave in?

He jumped from the bed and dressed. He pulled his hair into a queue then turned to Kyndra's cuff still lying on the bed. He refused to leave it, but neither would it fit his arm.

His lips parted as he swore he saw one of the eyes shift. Could it be that it held some magic? Dare he hope?

Aimery lifted it around to the back of his head where he threaded his hair through it. He smiled when the cuff changed, growing smaller to wrap around his hair. There wasn't a lot of magic in the cuff, but there might just be enough to help Kyndra.

He strode to the door and jerked it open. Only to find his weapons lying in the corridor. Aimery glanced first one way then the other before he bent and retrieved his sword and dagger. He strapped his weapons on and flexed his hand. It seemed Isran wanted a battle, and it was a fight Aimery was certainly looking forward to.

"Which way are you?" he murmured.

Aimery decided to turn right. He walked the silent hallway for a time seeing no one, hearing nothing. Most of the torches had burned out, darkening the passage. He unsheathed his dagger and stepped carefully. When he came to a corner, he flattened himself against the wall before he rounded the turn, weapon raised.

He had expected Isran to place men in his way, to prolong him and tire him. And without his magic, Aimery would have to be careful that he didn't expend too much of himself before he meet Isran.

When he came to a set of stairs he looked down first then glanced up and saw a guard waiting for him. Aimery smiled. He was ready for a fight. He moved his dagger to his left hand and unsheathed his sword as he took the stairs two at a time.

The guard had the advantage of being higher up than Aimery, but Aimery wasn't concerned. He ducked when the guard swung the sword at his head, and he lunged up the stairs as he straightened, plunging his dagger into the man's stomach.

Aimery pushed the dead guard off his blade and cautiously continued up the stairway. He had climbed two more levels when the next attack came. Aimery heard them just before he turned the corner on the landing. He fell down onto one knee to avoid a swing of a sword. The blade embedded into the rock, giving Aimery the time he needed to slice the guard's neck as he stood.

It was just a whisper of movement and instinct that made Aimery duck and roll. He jumped to his feet and turned to find two more guards waiting for him.

"I suppose you want the same fate as your comrade, aye?" he taunted them.

The man on the left lunged at Aimery. Aimery blocked the blow of the war ax with his sword the same time he kicked the second guard in the balls. As the second bent over with a wail of pain, Aimery twisted around the first guard until his sword was against his neck.

"You can either drop your weapon and live, or you can die."

The guard elbowed him in the ribs as an answer.

Aimery plunged his dagger into the man's side. "Wrong choice."

With two guards lying dead at his feet, he turned to the one still rolling around on the floor clutching his balls. "I'll give you the same option I just gave your friend."

The second guard pulled himself up on his hands and knees and crawled away. Aimery blew out a breath and turned to the next flight of stairs. Where did they lead? And what did Isran have waiting for him next?

Aimery didn't have long to find out. On the next landing five men waited for him. He eyed the men, determining how he was going to kill them. One laughed, swinging his blade around him as he stepped toward Aimery.

"We was told ye were a mighty warrior."

Aimery shrugged. "I did get past the others."

All five men chuckled.

"Aye," the first one said. "But ye won't be gettin' past us."

Aimery didn't have time to talk. He lunged forward, his sword sinking into the man. The guard's startled eyes widened before they closed. Aimery kicked the man off his sword and beckoned the others forward.

They didn't hesitate. He stepped to the side, making one trip over their dead comrade. Another moved behind him, just as he wanted. Aimery elbowed him in the nose which sent him staggering backwards, his arms flailing as he tumbled down the stairs.

The other two came at him with their swords swinging. Aimery used both his sword and his dagger to block their swings and get in some swings of his own. The third had finally found his feet, though he was covered in the dead guard's blood.

Aimery grabbed the third man and turned just as the other two drove their blades toward him. The third grunted as the weapons sunk into him, blood bubbling from his mouth as his life drained away. Aimery pushed him away and spun. He swung back with his dagger, finding the spine of one while his sword sliced the other's neck.

He stood panting, his weapons dripping with blood. The need to find Kyndra, to make sure she was unharmed, was strong. Yet, he knew it was a trap. But a trap he had to walk into if he was going to save her.

After a deep breath, he started up the next flight of stairs.

Chapter Twenty-One

Isran could hardly contain his glee. Everything he had worked for, everything he had wanted was about to be his. He had known killing the dragon would propel Aimery to come after him, but he hadn't expected the priestess. She was a nice boon.

Not to mention she made controlling Aimery that much easier. If not for her, it would have been much more difficult to have everything come together. As it was, he had nearly lost Aimery to the madness. And he needed Aimery as sane as possible. At least for the time being.

Isran bit back a laugh and rubbed his hands together. He wanted to hurry the sun along its course, but he made himself be patient. If he couldn't stay in control now, everything would be lost. Forever.

There was no way he would return to the Realm of the Fae to face charges and punishment. He would end up in the Realm of Shadows and, though he liked to think he was stronger than Lugus, he wasn't so sure he could withstand the realm for even a day.

I won't have to. I've got the egg and the priestess. And I'm about to have the greatest warrior the Fae has ever known on my side.

"I wouldn't gloat too soon."

He turned his head to find Kyndra walking toward him. She was a vision with her dark locks curled around her and the crimson gown hugging her voluptuous frame. By the time this night was over, she would be in his bed. Every thought of Aimery would be banished from her mind.

"Do you know how long I've planned this?"

She shrugged. "Do you think I care?"

The way she lifted her brows in defiance, as if she dared him to challenge her, told him that she had submersed herself in the black magic. He reached out with his mind and tested her. "Ah, your magic has grown."

"As you said, it's easy to give into the seduction of the dark side."

"So I did." He smiled and ran his fingers down her face. "Do you know what you need to do for the ceremony?"

"Of course."

He studied her, wondering if she had the nerve to try and deceive him. He could feel the black magic within her, hungering for more, but a part of him cautioned him against her. As beautiful as she was, she had been Aimery's and a priestess. It took more than a day to erase all of that.

But a day had been all he had. Even then, it had taken everything he had to give her that day. Had he pushed her, she would have broken, leaving him with no priestess and nothing with which to leverage against Aimery. So he had wasted a day, a day when he could have been conquering other realms.

It was only a day. Just one day when a forever stretched before him.

Isran took in a deep breath and grinned. "Aye, you know the ceremony. Will your magic be strong enough though?"

"What do you think I've been doing for the past several hours but strengthening my magic?"

He bent his head toward her neck. Instead of turning away as she had before, she tilted her head to the side. Desire flared through him. "Eternity is before us, Kyndra. Will you stand by my side?" he asked before he nuzzled her neck.

"For a price."

He straightened. "Name it."

"Oh, I will when the time comes."

"It wouldn't have anything to do with Aimery, now would it?" He would give her anything but him.

She shook her head. "You want Aimery for yourself."

"I do. I have plans for me."

"Will he join us?"

Isran smiled and tapped her lips with his fingers. "That, my sweet, is a secret. Tell me what you want?"

"In time, my lord. In time."

"I don't like surprises." In fact, he hated them.

"You'll like this one. I promise," she whispered seductively.

Isran wanted to pull her into his arms, to cover her mouth with his, but he held himself still. It wasn't time for him to claim her. The sun still shown in the sky. But once darkness fell, once she had broken the egg and begun the ceremony, once he had his power, then he would claim her, pounding into her delectable body until she was too sore to move.

Just thinking of taking her made his cock swell and his balls tighten. He wanted to cover her dark nipples with his mouth and savor the little buds as they hardened. He wanted to lick her sex, to taste her as she peaked.

It had been hell watching her and Aimery make love. For so long Aimery had been everything he wanted to be. Now he would have something that Aimery had. He would take it away from Aimery and make it his. Already he had turned Kyndra, but he had to be careful to keep her with him.

"I'd prefer if you told me what you wanted now."

Kyndra shrugged a slender shoulder. "That's too bad."

It was then he realized she wasn't wearing the rubies. He had enchanted them, making them so alluring that she would never want to take them off and thereby binding her to him always so there could never be a chance of Aimery coming between them.

"Why aren't you wearing the necklace I left for you?"

"The rubies?" she asked. "I didn't want to."

"But I would prefer that you did."

Her lips turned up into a smile. "Then I'm going to have to disappoint you, Isran, because I'm not wearing them."

"Why?"

"I just don't want to."

Could she be powerful enough already to withstand his enchantment on the necklace? A thrill of excitement rushed through him at the prospect. "Then don't. It matters not."

She narrowed her gaze at him. "What did you want me for? I was having fun delving deeper into the black magic."

"The sun is sinking rapidly. I want to make sure all is as it should be."

"Then let us prepare. Where is the egg?"

He lifted a brow. "Hidden."

"I thought you wanted to prepare."

"There's no need to bring out the egg before it's time. I don't want it to be…damaged…in any way."

"You don't trust me."

It wasn't a question. He glanced at her lips that had formed into a tantalizing pout. "You must earn my trust, my sweet."

"When I crack open that egg and perform the ceremony, I suppose."

"Quite right."

She flung her hair over her shoulder and turned away from him. "You have no need for me as of yet, then. I'm going to continue my…practice."

Isran watched the gentle sway of her hips as she left. There was nothing to prepare, he had just wanted to see her. He would bring the egg only when it was time. The dagger Kyndra would use was already on the altar.

Other than Aimery, Kyndra and himself, all was set.

He leisurely walked around the top of the tower. The center

of the coned roof had been left open, which made it a perfect place for his ritual. The tower wasn't the largest in the castle, but it was the tallest. He wanted Aimery close, but not too close. Not yet, anyway.

Isran paused beside the door Kyndra had exited and wondered how soon Aimery would make it to the top. The guards he had placed throughout the castle had merely been done to tire Aimery. He was too fine a fighter, even without his powers, to be bested by any of Isran's guards.

But a powerless Aimery, exhausted from numerous battles, just what Isran wanted. Only then would all his plans come to fruition.

Aimery knelt and retrieved his dagger from the dead guard. He had lost count of the number he had killed, but all had refused to drop their weapons. Again and again they had attacked him.

He could feel himself weakening, and he hated it. He pushed onward, because he had no other choice. Aimery stood and rested his hands on his knees as he fought to calm his racing breath.

This must be how humans feel.

He chuckled as he thought of the humans he called friends. Many battles they had fought, and each time they had kept up with him, never complaining when their limbs tired or their breath burned their lungs.

Aimery had taken his magic for granted, but never again. Once he got them back—and he would get them back—he was going to appreciate every day he woke to feel the magic thrumming through him.

He straightened and glanced upward. There one, maybe two, more flights of stairs as far as he could tell. Once at the top, he had no doubt he would find Isran soon enough.

Aimery climbed the stairs and cast a glance out of the narrow slit in the stones to find the sun nearly buried in the horizon. He had been fighting most of the day with no nourishment. His stomach growled, but more than anything he longed for a cool drink of water.

Instead, he found more guards. The two who blocked his path were large, brawny men. By the size of their hands they could crush a man's skull.

"You know," Aimery said as he stopped at the landing. "I've never liked the silly red turbans that you wear. Is your hair so awful that all of you must hide it?"

One of the guards, he couldn't tell which, growled in response. Not that he had expected an answer. The men had more muscles than brains, and these two would tire him out much more than all the others combined.

He thought of Kyndra, of her sweet smile and her smell of jasmine and sunshine. It renewed him, giving him the vigor he needed to duck as the two came at him. He passed beneath the two meaty fists they had aimed at his face. They used no other weapons than their hands, but it was enough that Aimery knew he had to stay out of their reach.

But that proved more difficult than he had imagined.

He staggered back against the wall as one of the guards slammed a fist into his jaw. Aimery wasn't sure if it was broken or not, and there wasn't time to test it as the second fist swung at him.

Aimery ducked and rolled. He came up in time to see the guard's fist land in the stones. Aimery grimaced at hearing the crunch of bone, but the guard didn't make a sound.

"Shite," Aimery murmured as he climbed to his feet.

He reached for his sword when the second guard's arms wrapped around him, trapping his arms against him. Aimery kicked and struggled to get free, but the guard's hold didn't budge.

The first chuckled as he slammed a fist into Aimery's stomach. All the air left Aimery's lungs as he blinked and struggled to stay conscious. He jerked back and planted his feet in the chest of the first guard which sent him stumbling backwards. It gave Aimery the time he needed to throw back his head into the guard that held him.

There was a muffled curse before the guard's hold loosened and Aimery dropped to his feet. He twisted on one knee and shoved his sword into the guard. As the second came at him again, Aimery pulled his weapon free and ducked under the guard's fist. When he stood up, he stepped back and thrust his blade into the man's back.

He knew he needed to continue moving on, but he had to rest. A stitch had begun in his side, and he tried to swallow, but all his spit was gone. He turned his back to the wall and rested against it. There were no more stairs to climb, only a long, dark corridor ahead of him.

His arms felt as though they were chained to the stones. It took all his effort just to lift his hand and wipe away the sweat from his brow. He was in no condition to fight Isran, and Isran knew it.

Anger infused him. He had lived through thousands of millennia to die because he had no magic and he was tired. The irony was laughable, if he could find the energy to smile. As it was, the only thing keeping Aimery going was Kyndra.

He pushed off the wall and started down the hallway. Each step became harder and harder until Aimery had to use the wall to keep upright. He hated the weakness that had taken over his body, the bruises and aches that he had never felt for more than a heartbeat while he had his magic.

He paused and leaned his cheek against the cool stones. Blood coated his weapons and him, but he paid it no heed. It was a part of battle. Remembering the dragon cuff that had wound itself around his queue, he sheathed his dagger and reached back to touch it.

A shock, like lightning, pierced his finger and raced through him. He sucked in a breath as renewed strength and energy consumed him. Aimery stood still as stone for a moment as he tried to take in what had just happened.

Kyndra had never spoken of the cuff as magic, but he

hadn't imagined what had just occurred. He knew it had been magic that flowed through him and, though he didn't know how, he welcomed it.

Aimery took a deep breath and continued down the corridor until it ended at the base of a staircase that wound upward to a tower. Somehow, he wasn't surprised. Isran always liked to make a grand entrance. What better way to show all of Thav that they had a new king than at the top of a tower.

"By all that's magical, give me strength," Aimery murmured as he started up the stairs.

Chapter Twenty-Two

Kyndra watched the sun sink below the horizon casting the land in a somber gray. She had held out hope that Aimery would come for her, that he would somehow manage to get to her before dusk. But he hadn't.

She didn't blame him though. Isran had hinted that he had something special planned for Aimery, and she doubted that meant a special meal. Isran might admire Aimery, but she had never seen someone so jealous of another before. Isran wanted to be Aimery and, when he couldn't, he decided to be better. No matter the price.

One of the giant birds that had chased her and Aimery that first night flew by the window. It called loudly, the sound forlorn and almost...lost. A lot like the way she was, Kyndra mused inwardly.

She was lost. She had not only forsaken the Order for her love for Aimery, but she had betrayed every Fae by turning to the black magic. There was no doubt the magic running through her now was powerful indeed. It was heady to feel the magic infuse her, pump through her very veins. She could do things that she had never been able to before. The knowledge that came with the power was disturbing and exhilarating.

With every breath she took she delved deeper into the dark side, learning the magic, controlling it. She could feel herself growing more powerful. Once she accepted what she had done, knowing it could save Aimery, she had given herself up to it wholly.

Kyndra walked around the spacious tower. It was the tallest of the castle and, once the ceremony was completed, the light that would shine from Isran would light the realm. Her new realm.

Isran had made it clear he wanted her, and she would let him think he could have her. She would even give him her body if it meant she could earn his trust. But one day, when he trusted her fully, she would kill him.

She stopped near the stone slab where a single dagger was placed. It was the weapon she would use to crack open the egg. It tore at her heart to kill a being she had spent her life helping and loving, but there was no way around it.

Kyndra lifted the dagger and inspected the blade. Near the hilt it was as wide as her palm and narrowed down to a point. It glistened in the candlelight. She lifted a hand and touched the pad of her finger on the blade. Blood welled from the spot and ran down her palm. There was no pain, and the wound healed almost immediately.

"It's time."

She looked up to find Isran standing on the other side of the altar. He had removed his tunic and boots and stood only in his black breeches. His flaxen hair hung loose about his bare shoulders, lifting in the soft wind.

"Where is the egg?"

Isran grinned. "In just a moment, my sweet. We have one more that we're waiting for."

Kyndra's heart accelerated. Surely he wasn't talking about Aimery. She had taken steps to make sure Aimery would never see her overtaken by the dark side.

There was a sound at the door and, when she turned, her gaze locked with Aimery.

Nay!

Aimery kept his expression blank. He had known Kyndra would be with Isran. He just hadn't expected to find that the woman he loved had sided with such a bastard. He hadn't just failed the dragons and his realm, he had failed Kyndra and his vow to her.

He struggled to breathe as he gazed upon her beauty. The crimson gown was striking on her. He wanted nothing more than to take her in his arms and kiss her until they were both breathless.

But he would never have her again.

Isran stepped into his line of vision. Aimery raised a brow at him.

"You're much haler than I expected you to be," Isran said with a smirk. "Did you choose to run away instead of fighting my men?"

"Go have a look yourself."

Isran's swirling gaze narrowed. "You've had no sustenance, Aimery, and you've been battling for more than half the day. You should be crawling up those steps, not standing here arguing with me."

Aimery couldn't stop the smile that pulled at his lips. "I would apologize for disappointing you, Isran, but I really could give a shite. I'm stronger than you realized."

"And your madness?"

"It's amazing what a battle can do to clear your head." Isran didn't need to know that he had nearly fallen into his insanity several times when his body had begun to tire.

"For all your words, you are exhausted. I can see the light fading from your eyes, the way your fingers are barely holding onto your weapon, and how you need to lean against the door to keep your footing."

Aimery shrugged. "I'm sick of hearing you talk. Get on with whatever you wanted me for."

"Oh, you know why you're here. It's time to crack the egg."

"What do you need me for? It looks as though you already have an assistant."

Isran put his hands behind his back and smiled. "She's lovely, isn't she? I knew the moment I saw her she was your weakness."

"I know you plan to use her against me."

"Do you now? And how do you think I'm going to do that?"

Aimery shrugged. "You've turned her to your side obviously."

"That was obvious, wasn't it?"

"What I want to know is why? You could have used our realm, Theron, or any number of things to bend me to your will."

Isran leaned close and whispered, "Because what I have in store for you called for something…special."

Aimery's blood turned to ice at Isran's words. He dared not look at Kyndra. It was enough that she was standing with Isran. And not him. Isran was close enough for an attack, his defenses were down. Aimery didn't hesitate as he stepped from the wall and thrust his sword at Isran.

The bastard threw back his head and laughed. "Come, come, Aimery. I anticipated you would do something this foolish."

Aimery stared at his sword that had stopped inches from Isran's stomach. He willed his arm to move, to kill Isran before it was too late. But Isran had outmaneuvered him. The last of his strength had gone into the attack, and it was by sheer will alone that he didn't crumple on the floor.

"Now will you bend to me?"

Aimery glared at him. "Never."

"Oh, you will. Never doubt that."

The sword was yanked out of his hand by Isran's magic and smashed against the wall, shattering into dust. The next instant

Aimery was slammed against the stone wall, his arms stretched out at his sides.

"This will be a perfect place for you to watch," Isran said.

Aimery jerked at the invisible bonds. He hung several feet off the floor, powerless to do anything other than watch, just as Isran wanted.

Unable to keep his gaze from her any longer, Aimery looked at Kyndra. She followed Isran with her eyes as if he were the only one in the world who mattered to her. It was like a dagger in his heart. Their nights together had meant more to him than to her. It had been a chance he'd taken and, even now, he didn't regret a moment of it.

He loved her. It was something he had thought never to happen to him and, now that it had, he would be denied even that. He was touted as their realm's finest warrior, but that didn't grant him the love he had wanted above all else.

"Have you ever seen a dragon's egg, Aimery?" Isran asked.

He didn't bother to respond. Isran didn't really want an answer. He just wanted to hear himself talk.

"Let me show you one." Isran snapped his fingers and a large, pale blue egg appeared in front of him.

The egg stood nearly as tall as Isran, luminous in the light of the candles. Aimery was in awe. He had glimpsed the egg when he had looked through the male dragon's eyes, but it was different than seeing it himself.

"Magnificent, isn't it?" Isran murmured. He ran his hand over the egg as if caressing it. "I planned this moment for thousands of years. All my plans revolved around you, Aimery."

Aimery clenched his jaw. "Why was I the special one? I'm the one who befriended you."

Isran chuckled. "Why do you think I sought out your friendship? Everyone knows who Aimery is. Everyone reveres you, whispers about you as if you were a god instead of just a commander."

"So you spent the next thousand years learning everything I

could teach you."

"It was easy. I became what you wanted me to be, and in return I got to see parts of the palace others never did."

"Why kill the other Fae?"

Isran shrugged. "They had the misfortune of discovering me while I was practicing my magic, my…black magic. I couldn't very well let them run off and tell you or Theron. I wasn't prepared yet. They had to die."

"You did all of this just to get me here. Why? Because you hate me so?"

"I don't know that I would call it hate," Isran said as he walked in front of the egg. "If not for a quirk of fate, your life could have been mine."

"Because fate chose me, I get punished for it."

"Not at all, brother. I'm going to reward you."

Aimery laughed, the sound echoing around the tower. "You call this a reward?"

"Well, I admit, there will be some pain before the reward. But afterward, it is well and truly a reward. Just ask your lover, though she isn't yours any longer."

Aimery clenched his jaw when Kyndra raised her gaze to his. There was something different about her. He had sensed it the night before, but now it was more pronounced, almost as if…

"Kyndra, nay," he said with a groan. "Tell me you aren't using black magic."

Isran clapped. "I wondered how long it would take you to realize it. Not even last night when you had your hands and mouth on her body did you realize it."

"You watched, you sick son of a bitch?"

"Aye, I did. Too bad I won't let you do the same when I claim her tonight."

Aimery yanked with all his might against the unseen chains, but he didn't budge.

"Kyndra has a weakness as well," Isran said.

"The dragons, I know."

"Nay, not the dragons. Imagine my surprise when I learned you were her weakness."

Aimery stilled and looked at Kyndra. A single tear rolled down her cheek. She had turned for him. For *him*! She could never return to their realm, never know the dragons again. Everything she had been was lost. Gone forever.

It was more than Aimery could take. He threw back his head and bellowed.

Chapter Twenty-Three

Kyndra shivered at the roar that sounded from Aimery. She realized too late that Isran hadn't wanted her, could have cared less if she had come to his side. He had done everything to put Aimery in this situation. Because he wanted *Aimery* to turn to the dark side.

It was so very clear, now that it was too late.

She had never felt like such a fool. She should have been able to see through Isran to realize what he was about. Aimery had even warned her and, though she knew Isran was using him against her, she had never dreamed he would go to these links.

"What are you going to do to him?" she asked.

Isran was smiling madly as he turned to her. "He's going to be joining us, my sweet. He will do anything to keep you away from me."

Kyndra clasped her hands behind her back to hide how they shook. Her soul was already damned, but Aimery's wasn't. She had to get to him, to talk to him before Isran converted him.

She licked her lips as she recalled the confusion then heartache in Aimery's beautiful eyes as he realized what she had become. He hated her now, she realized that, but that didn't stop her love for him.

"Is that a tear?"

She sniffed and arched a brow. "He's hurting my ears. Besides, I wonder if he will be the warrior he was after all of this."

"He'll be better than before."

She let out the breath she'd been holding when Isran turned his back to her. He had bought the lie, but she would have to be careful. Now that Isran had Aimery he didn't need her. He could kill her with just a thought, and she couldn't let that happen until she had spoken to Aimery.

With a lick of her lips she walked to the egg. Aimery's bellow ripped through her soul, his anger and frustration palpable. When he finally quieted, she glanced at him over her shoulder to find his head hanging between his shoulders as though he had passed out. "He'll be fine," Isran assured her.

"He better be."

Isran wrapped his arm around her and brought her against him. "Do you want to touch the egg?"

She did, but she couldn't, not knowing that she would be killing it in a few moments. "Nay."

"Are you ready to begin the ceremony?"

"What of Aimery?"

"I can wake him up quick enough."

Kyndra walked to Aimery, wondering if Isran would let her get close enough. She was concerned about Aimery. He had held on to his sanity by a thin ribbon that could have unraveled. "What if he's fallen into madness?"

She stopped in front of him. "Aimery?" she whispered.

He didn't respond.

"He's safe enough," Isran called. "Nothing can break those chains."

"Aimery, please," she hissed. "Tell me you are still with me."

"So you can torment me more?" Aimery asked.

She let out a sigh. "Thank the gods."

"Why?"

He had lifted his gaze to stare at her. She lost herself in his swirling blue eyes. "He wants you to turn to the dark side. Don't do it. No matter what he says, please. My soul is damned. Don't condemn yours as well."

"Is he awake?" Isran asked.

"Please," she mouthed. "Aye, my lord. He's awake."

"And sane?"

Kyndra fisted her hands to keep from touching Aimery. His face was bruised, though not as she would have expected. It was almost as if he possessed some magic. Then she caught the glint off of sapphire eyes at the back of his head.

My cuff.

"Kyndra! Is he sane?" Isran demanded.

She took a step back. "Hard to say, my lord."

Isran was by her side in a moment. "I need him sane."

"Maybe you shouldn't have pushed him so."

"I had to push him. He's strong, too strong to give into the madness so easily."

Kyndra turned and started back to the altar. That's when she spotted the missive Theron had written for them. She had forgotten about it, but why did Isran have it. For all he knew, it was simply a message.

While Isran was occupied with Aimery, Kyndra grabbed the rolled parchment and hurried around the altar. The dagger waited for her to pierce the egg, to begin Isran's transformation into the most powerful being in the entire universe. No one, not the Fae or the Draconians, would be able to defeat him.

Kyndra closed her eyes and listened to the knowledge inside her, searching for an answer she feared wasn't there.

Theron rubbed his tired eyes with his thumb and forefinger. He and Lugus had looked at the map of Thav for hours with no clues as to how to get in undetected. Everything had been shoved off his desk so the map could be spread out. He leaned back in his chair and stared at the parchment.

"If there had been a way, that's how I would have brought Aimery and Kyndra to begin with," Lugus said.

"I know. I just can't help thinking we're missing something. "

"Isran will be waiting for us to bring in the army. He knows how much Aimery means to the realm."

Theron shook his head. "I want to go in and save Aimery."

"But you can't. If anyone is going, it's me."

"Ahryn would never forgive me."

"We either wait for Isran to attack us, or we go after Aimery."

"Nay," Rufina said from the doorway.

Both turned to face her. Theron rose as his wife walked toward him, one delicate hand on her stomach swollen with their second child. He took her hands and guided her to a chair. "You're supposed to be with our daughter."

"And you're supposed to include me on these schemes of yours." She turned her gaze to Lugus. "Ahryn would be furious if she knew."

Lugus held up his hands. "Easy, Rufina. Nothing has been decided. We're just talking."

"Neither of you can go into Thav," she said. "I told Theron from the first moment I met Isran I didn't care for him. He's too devious."

"That he is, my love," Theron murmured.

Lugus leaned forward in his chair and propped his elbows on his knees. "I can't leave Aimery to face whatever kind of hell Isran has planned for him."

"I don't think he wants Aimery for that," Rufina suggested as Theron helped her into a chair. "I think Isran wants Aimery to stand with him."

"By all that's magical." Theron swallowed and sank into his seat. "Aimery's power is great. If Isran can get him to turn to the dark…"

He couldn't finish the sentence, because just thinking it made his gut hurt.

"The army is ready," Lugus reminded him. "They're standing guard now, awaiting orders."

Rufina placed her hand atop Theron's. "I want to save Aimery, too, but we can't. We have to wait."

Theron looked from his queen to his brother. "I won't forgive myself if Aimery loses his life in this."

"Aimery is strong. He'll pull through." Lugus rose and walked to the window.

Theron prayed his brother was right.

Aimery wanted to stay in the pit of despair that had overtaken him. His madness, his insanity was better than what was happening around him.

But Kyndra's sweet voice had broken into his mind and called to him. He had wanted to ignore her, but there was something in her voice that made him open his eyes. She had turned to black magic, she had chosen to stand beside Isran, but in her beautiful swirling blue gaze he had seen the woman he had fallen in love with.

He'd been about to answer her when Isran decided to move beside her. Aimery hastily closed his eyes and focused on renewing his strength. The egg hadn't been broken yet, which meant there was a chance he could get to Isran.

"Aimery?" Isran called. "I went to too much trouble for you to lose yourself in your mind. "

Aimery didn't move.

Isran stepped closer. "What of Kyndra? Aren't you going to fight for her? I know you care for her. Perhaps you even…love her."

It took everything Aimery had not to open his eyes. He had never wanted to battle someone as fiercely as he did Isran. The lies, the betrayal and now Kyndra.

"I know you can hear me," Isran whispered. "Come out and play, Aimery."

Aimery cracked open an eye to see something in Kyndra's hand. He recognized the scroll in her hand as the missive Theron had given him. Why did she have it?

Her gaze lifted to his, and he spotted the dagger in her other hand.

"It's time," Isran shouted. "I'm ready to receive my power and rule the universe."

Aimery found it difficult to watch as Kyndra walked around the altar to stand beside the egg. Isran knelt in front of the egg, his head lifted and his arms opened wide.

"Come, Kyndra," he called. "Begin the ceremony."

Aimery no longer cared if Isran knew he was awake or not. His gaze was riveted on Kyndra. She had set the scroll behind the egg on the altar and raised the dagger over her head. Her lips moved as she began to chant in a voice that was more song than speech. The words were difficult to understand, as if she were channeling power from somewhere else.

He pulled at his invisible chains, urging the magic of the cuff to aid him. Of a sudden, he dropped to the floor, balancing on the balls of his foot and his hands. Isran was too occupied with Kyndra to realize he had gotten free. Aimery had to stop Kyndra. The egg couldn't be broken, Isran couldn't bath in the yolk and, above all else, Kyndra couldn't complete the ceremony.

Aimery pulled his dagger from its sheath and readied it to throw at Kyndra. The thought of killing her made him ill, but he had no other choice. It wasn't just the Fae realm in danger, but every realm in the universe. He had an obligation, regardless of his feelings toward Kyndra, to stop them in whatever way necessary.

The metal from the dagger was cool in his hand. He wanted to aim for her heart, but she was turned to the side. The only spot available to him that would give her a quick death was the neck.

Her eyes flew open, and she arched her back. Aimery lifted his arm, ready to throw the dagger. He reared back just before she plunged the weapon into the egg. As he moved his arm forward to throw the dagger, he realized her blade had missed the egg and sunk into the seal on the scroll.

Aimery turned his hand to make sure the dagger missed Kyndra. He jumped to his feet as lightning filled the room, striking him again and again. Only it wasn't pain he felt, but magic, beautiful, pure magic.

Kyndra smiled as she saw the magic pour into Aimery. He had freed himself from the chains and, by the dagger sunk into the stones behind her, he had intended to kill her. Yet, it didn't matter. Aimery stood with his head thrown back and his arms out wide as the magic struck him repeatedly.

"You bitch," Isran shouted and jumped to his feet.

Kyndra didn't run. She might not have the power to defeat him, but she would battle him until Aimery was able to take over. She wasn't expecting his hand to connect with her cheek.

"That is the first and last time you will betray me," he snarled.

"Do your worst."

He smirked. "And I know just the thing," he said as he raised his palms toward her.

Kyndra screamed as the fire flew from his hands and surrounded her. She glanced at Aimery. The fire ate away at her, sucking her life force until she couldn't fight the darkness closing in around her.

"Aimery," she whispered just before the light went out.

Chapter Twenty-Four

Aimery fell to his knees, his breathing ragged. The tower was quiet, too quiet. He looked up to find Isran enclosing Kyndra in a ball of flame. He rose and started toward her, when Isran's voice stopped him cold.

"Move another step toward me and I kill her."

Aimery glanced at Kyndra. "What are you doing to her?"

Isran shrugged and faced him. "I could kill her with just a thought. For now, she's my prisoner. The fire is made of pure magic. Try to touch it, and it'll burn you."

Kyndra looked as if she were asleep, but Aimery wanted her out of the fireball before Isran did kill her. Magic rushed through him, demanding he let it loose. But Aimery held fast and waited. Isran was confident, mayhap too confident. Aimery would use it to his advantage when the time came.

"What? No witty remark?" Isran taunted. "I would have thought you'd be on your knees begging me for her life."

"Why, when it's me you want?"

Isran chuckled and shook his head. "I always thought you were more intelligent than any Fae I knew, but you've proven that I was wrong. You're thinking with your cock instead of your mind."

"What would you know about it? The only way you could get a woman into your bed was through magic." Just as Aimery expected, Isran's lip curled in fury. "Did I make you angry?"

"I can see I was wrong about you. You aren't the warrior I want by my side when I take over the universe."

"*If* you take over the universe," Aimery corrected.

Isran growled and took a step to the left. Aimery moved with him. They circled each other, each waiting for the other to strike. Aimery wasn't sure what kind of magic was inside him, but he knew it was strong. Possibly strong enough to defeat even Isran.

"You know I'm going to kill you."

Aimery shrugged and halted. "Maybe. Maybe not. I'm ready to find out."

"Suit yourself."

Aimery used his magic and called a sword to each hand and swung them around himself. The blades glowed blue and sung as they sliced through the air.

"Impressive," Isran said with raised brows. The next instant he held two swords with flames as blades. "Where did you get the magic?"

"It's a secret."

"One I intend to discover."

Aimery shook his head as they began to circle each other again. "That was always your problem, Isran. Everything you wanted was in your grasp, you just didn't want to work toward it."

"Why work for it when I can get it for free."

"Because the cost is your soul."

Isran threw back his head and laughed. "Do you think you can kill me? The Fae you called brother?"

"In a heartbeat."

Aimery ducked as Isran stepped toward him and swung the sword at his head. Aimery straightened and pivoted, slicing downward. He grinned when Isran yelped in pain and blood ran down his leg from the cut across his thigh.

"Does it hurt?"

Isran's lips peeled back in a sneer. "You will pay for that."

Aimery brought his left arm up, using his sword to block a downward swing from Isran's weapon. His right arm jerked up to halt the thrust of Isran's second blade, but still the point of the sword penetrated his thigh.

"An eye for an eye," Isran said as he stepped back.

Aimery's leg felt as if it were on fire. He glanced down at the tear in his breeches and grimaced when he saw the scorch marks on his skin and clothes.

"Does it hurt?" Isran mocked.

In answer, Aimery lunged toward Isran. One arm blocked Isran while the second thrust into his side. Isran howled in pain and spun away from him. Aimery barely had time to raise his swords to stop Isran's blades. Aimery jerked his arm out and, with a flick of his wrist, nicked Isran's wrist so that his sword went flying to clatter on the stones across the tower.

Isran attacked, his sword a blur he moved it so deftly. Aimery hissed as he lost one of his swords. He ducked and rolled to his feet when Isran swung at his neck. As Aimery stood, a bolt of pain ran through his arm. When he looked, he saw Isran's blade sticking through his arm. Isran knocked Aimery's second sword from his hand, his laughter filling the tower.

"I thought you might last longer."

Aimery jerked his arm off Isran's blade and faced him. Isran thrust his blade, but Aimery gripped his wrist, stopping him instantly. Aimery turned and elbowed Isran in the face. The crack of bone shattered the silence. It felt so good Aimery did it a second time before he backhanded Isran.

Isran crumpled to his knees, blood pouring from his nose and lips. It wouldn't be long before he began to heal. Aimery reached for his sword and grasped Isran's shoulder.

"I did call you brother, but you must pay for your crimes."

Aimery knew the likelihood of getting Isran back to his realm was almost none. His punishment must be carried out now and, though Aimery was loath to do it, it was his duty. He reared back his arms as Isran's eyes widened. Before Isran could gather any magic, Aimery plunged the blade into his heart.

Isran clutched at Aimery's arm as his life faded from his eyes. He fell to the side, his gaze now on the egg. Aimery didn't want to watch him die, not someone he had thought of as family. He wanted back in his realm, with Kyndra in his arms.

He walked to Kyndra and laid his sword on the altar. Just as he reached for the fire that surrounded her Isran began to laugh. Aimery turned his head to look at him. There was a loud crack, and Aimery whirled around to see the egg shatter, spilling the yolk on the stones.

A glance at Isran confirmed that he was indeed dead, but Aimery wasn't about to take any chances. He rushed to Isran and tossed him onto the altar so the yolk couldn't touch him. Then he faced Kyndra.

The sphere of flames didn't diminish with Isran's death. Aimery gazed at Kyndra suspended in mid-air, her long, dark locks floating through the flames as if they were water. She had sacrificed everything. For him.

And he would do the same.

Aimery took a deep breath and stepped into the sphere. The flames licked at his skin, scorching him with burns that laced across his body like whip marks. He gathered Kyndra in his arms and hugged her to him.

"I'm sorry, my love. So sorry I failed you."

Aimery stepped out of the sphere and closed his eyes as he thought of his realm. In the next breath he found himself standing in a corridor of the palace. He smiled as he took in the beauty of the Fae. They had made it.

"Aimery?"

He looked up to find Theron and Lugus running toward

him.

Lugus was the first to reach him. "What happened to her?"

"I'll explain everything once she's settled."

"Is she dead?"

"Nay." Aimery could still feel her heart beating in her chest. It was power he had never had before, power he had never thought to experience.

"Come," Theron said. "There's a chamber for her."

But Aimery shook his head. "She's going to mine."

Theron and Lugus followed him to his chamber. After Aimery had her on his bed and covered, he motioned them out and closed the door behind him. He leaned his head against the door and sighed.

"You look like hell," Lugus murmured.

Aimery snorted. "I feel like it."

"Are those burns?"

He turned to Theron and nodded. "They are. Let's leave Kyndra in peace. I'll tell you everything over a feast and a case of wine."

An hour later Aimery pushed his platter away and leaned back in his chair with a goblet in hand. "That's all of it."

"By the gods," Theron murmured.

Lugus shook his head sadly. "She did all of that and still managed to survive? I thought once someone turned to the dark they were forever lost."

"Not all," Rufina said as she came into the chamber. She took the chair next to Theron and smiled at Aimery. "Kyndra didn't go willingly to black magic. It was forced upon her and, by what you've told us, it was love for you that kept her from turning evil."

Aimery wanted to believe Kyndra loved him, but he wasn't sure. He knew he loved her and that she cared for him, but was it love? "What will happen to her?"

"Nothing," Theron said. "She did exactly what you told her to—stay alive."

"Even though she used black magic."

Rufina sighed. "The use of black magic will be like a scar that she will carry the rest of her life."

Aimery was tired, both mentally and physically. His need to be with Kyndra had made him antsy the past hour, but he had owed Theron an explanation. Now that it was over, he couldn't stay away from Kyndra. He drained his goblet and rose. "I want out of these clothes and a hot bath."

He walked from the chamber, grateful none stopped him.

Chapter Twenty-Five

Kyndra took a deep breath and stretched. She opened her eyes to find herself staring at cerulean blue sheer bed hanging that draped around the four posts of the bed as well as through the canopy. She didn't have to ask to know that somehow Aimery had won, and it was his bed she was lying in.

Tears gathered in her eyes and fell from the corners. She had expected to be left on Thav as her punishment. Instead, she had been brought home where the magic of the dragons pulsed and thrived in the beautiful realm.

Kyndra rolled to her side and gazed out the window that looked over the mountains. In the distance she could see a dragon soaring through the air. Its call could be heard, even from that distance.

She longed to go to the Blues, to ask their forgiveness for failing them. She hadn't brought back Isran for them to punish nor had she brought back the egg. She didn't know what happened to the precious treasure, but she was sure Aimery would have brought it had he been able.

Yet she couldn't go to the Blues, nor could she go to the Order. She had forsaken all of them, betrayed her vows. It was not something the Order took lightly. Not to mention she had used black magic in ways that made her stomach roll just thinking about it.

She was glad she was alone, because she needed time to herself before she faced anyone, least of all Aimery. Kyndra rose from the bed and ripped the hated crimson gown from her body. She tossed it into the hearth before she walked to the bathing chamber and readied her bath.

On a chair next to the tub was a long, flowing gown of the palest blue and embroidered with silver thread along the hem and cuffs with the knot work of the Fae. Lying atop the gown was her cuff. She brushed away new tears and climbed into the tub.

After scrubbing her skin raw and washing her hair twice, she rose from the water and dried off. She wrapped the towel around her and sat on the small bench before the opened doors that led to the terrace as she combed her hair. How long she sat there, she wasn't sure. She had gotten lost in her thoughts of the dragons, the Order, Thav and Aimery. Despite everything, she didn't regret giving herself to Aimery. What had happened between them had been more than lust. Dare she call it love?

But it was lost to her now. Everything was lost to her now. As much as she loved her realm, she didn't belong there. She had done the ultimate sin by practicing black magic. That could never be forgiven. Never.

She sighed and set down the comb. Then she rose and let the towel drop to get dressed. She slipped the gown over her and let her fingers trace the knot work of silver along the curved neckline. She slipped on the shoes, but ignored the cuff. With a sigh, she turned to find the queen in the doorway. Kyndra started to curtsey, but Rufina halted her.

"There's no need for that," Rufina said with a smile. "How are you?"

Kyndra glanced away from the queen and her flaxen hair that hung over one shoulder to drape across her belly swollen with child.

"I cannot imagine what you went through, Kyndra. I can

see the pain in your eyes. Aimery told us what happened."

Kyndra turned her head away. She wanted to leave the room, but no one left the king or queen without permission.

"He's been by your side these three days that you've slept. Only when we've made him has he left you. He cares a great deal about you, and I know he'll be ecstatic to learn you're awake."

She wasn't ready to face Aimery. What could she say? He had seen her at her worst.

"Will you tell me what happened?"

Kyndra shook her head. "There isn't much to tell, your highness. I used black magic and sided with Isran."

"Aimery tells me you did it for him."

She knew Aimery would say what he could to save her, but there was nothing that could save her. Not now. "Aimery doesn't know what he's talking about."

"Is that so?"

Kyndra whirled around to face Aimery who stood on the terrace. Gone were the black clothes Isran had made him wear, and in their place were dark blue breeches and a white tunic with dark blue knot work down the front from his shoulders to the hem.

"I'm not ready for this," she said and backed away.

"Ready for what? To see me? To hear that you did what you had to do?"

"Aimery, please. Stop."

He shook his head. "Nay. You could have plunged the dagger in the egg, but you didn't. You used it on the seal of the missive. How did you know there was magic in it?"

"I saw it glow blue."

"You saved me," he murmured. "You saved the realm."

She wanted to run, but she was trapped with Aimery in front of her and Rufina behind her. Every time she tried to use her magic to leave the palace, she felt Theron's magic stopping her.

"I'm not the person you think I am." She shrugged. "I

willingly joined Isran."

"If that's so, why did you bring me back from the madness again and again? Why didn't you crack the egg? Why did you help me?"

She saw the love shining in Aimery's eyes, and she longed to rush into his arms and feel them around her, sheltering her from everything. But she couldn't do that to him. He deserved someone who hadn't killed, who hadn't delved deep into the darkness.

"I wanted the power for myself. I wanted to take Isran's place. I had no idea the power would go to you."

"That's not true," Theron said from beside his wife. "Aimery got the magic Lugus and I put into the missive because you wanted him to have it."

Kyndra closed her eyes and tried again to leave. She wanted to be alone, to leave the realm forever. When she opened her eyes Aimery stood breaths from her.

"Deny it all you want, but your body knows."

She opened her lips to argue, but was silenced when Aimery's mouth covered hers. She couldn't stop the moan as he ravaged her mouth. One hand cupped the back of her head with the other wrapped around her, molding her to his hard body. Kyndra was powerless to do anything other than give herself up to the kiss. She had dreamed of his kisses, yearned for them as a Fae would yearn for magic.

He ended the kiss and smiled down at her. "Tell me your body doesn't hunger for mine. Tell me you don't dream about the nights we had together. Tell me you don't love me."

She couldn't. And he knew it. "Don't do this. You should never have returned me here."

"What was I supposed to do, leave you in Thav?"

"I might not be able to control my body, but I can prevent you from making a mistake."

"My love for you isn't a mistake."

She blinked back more tears. "You might not think so now, but you will. When people refuse to meet my eye on the street, no one will talk to you because I used black magic, or the Order stands against me you will regret it."

"Never."

But she wouldn't let him find out. She turned to face Theron and Rufina. "Please, let me leave. I cannot stay here."

"Where will you go?" Rufina asked.

"I need to be alone."

Theron gave a brief nod, and she hurried to leave before Aimery could stop her. As she faded from the palace, she heard him shout her name.

"Damn you, Theron," Aimery bellowed. "How could you do that?"

"She didn't want to stay, and you cannot make her."

"I could have made her see that she was wrong."

Rufina touched his arm, her smile sad. "Kyndra needs to see that on her own. Give her the time, Aimery. If it's meant to be, she'll come back to you."

"What if she doesn't?"

Rufina glanced at Theron. "Only time will tell."

Aimery ran a hand through his hair as the royal pair left his chambers. He walked to the terrace and stood in the doorway. He couldn't follow Kyndra now. Her magic was gone from the palace. She could be anywhere in the realm—or out of it. He had seen the fear in her gaze, the look of a trapped animal that seeks escape.

"I'm sorry, Aimery."

He shrugged, not bothering to turn and look at Lugus. "It went against everything in me to let her go. I fear I might have lost her forever."

"Do you love her?"

Aimery nodded and faced Lugus. "I'd die for her."

"Do you believe she loves you?"

"I do. She showed me with everything she did on Thav."

"Then give her time, my friend. "

"Would you have returned to Ahryn when you ran away?"

Lugus ran a hand over his chin. "I hadn't planned on it. I figured she would be better off without me, just as Kyndra feels toward you. She's giving up any happiness she might find to ensure that you don't regret being with her."

"What made you return to Ahryn?"

One side of Lugus' mouth lifted in a grin. "She did. She didn't give up on me."

Aimery nodded for now he knew what he had to do.

Chapter Twenty-Six

Kyndra brought her knees up to her chest and wrapped her arms around her legs. She had always loved the view from the top of the mountains. She dare not go near the Quay of Skulls and the blue dragons, but she was close enough that she could watch them.

She was glad to have left the palace. It had been nearly a week, and she had expected each day to get easier without Aimery. When in fact, it had gotten harder. To make matters worse, a part of her had longed for Aimery to come after her and drag her back to the palace. In the end, she knew she had done the right thing for them both.

For now she would stay in the realm, but she knew she would have to leave eventually. There were some Fae who made their homes in the mountains far away from others, but Kyndra didn't know how long she could stay away from the dragons. To live without them seemed impossible, but it was something she would have to do.

"I'm so sorry," she whispered into the wind.

The wind began to pick up, and she rose to her feet. She had spent all morning watching the dragons. There was a temple for the Order not too far from where she was, and she longed to visit it, to see Julieth and apologize for everything. But to go to the temple would be a death sentence to her.

Kyndra left the top of the mountain to travel the rolling hills. The grass stood to her waist, blowing gently in the wind, and the sun was high in the cloudless sky. Another perfect day in the realm.

A heartbeat before she saw the massive shadow she heard the beating of the dragon's wings. Kyndra stopped in her tracks as the female Blue dropped in front of her. She had never known a dragon to kill a Fae, but none had ever failed the dragons as she had.

If she were to die, the Blue had the right to kill her. Kyndra spread her arms to the side and closed her eyes as she waited for the dragon to breathe its fire on her. Instead, the dragon wrapped its claws around her and lifted her in the air as it flew to the Quay of Skulls.

Kyndra gripped the claws as the dragon took her straight up the sky until she couldn't make out the mountains anymore. Then the female rolled onto its back and tucked its wings against her before she plummeted, head first, back to the ground. A scream lodged itself in Kyndra's throat as her breath was stolen from her. The mountains grew closer and closer and, just before the dragon slammed into the rocks, she opened her wings and soared to the side.

With her heart pounding in her chest, Kyndra made herself loosen her hold on the dragon's claws. The dragon could let her go at any time, but she held on to Kyndra. Whatever fear Kyndra might have had melted away as the dragon soared over the lakes, rivers, mountains and valleys. It was a sight Kyndra would never forget.

But the time the female landed at her lair, Kyndra wasn't sure what the female wanted with her. She stumbled out of the dragon's claws and tilted her head back to look at the female. The dragon lowered her head until she could look Kyndra in the eye. Steam rolled from the dragon's nostrils as the sun glinted off the beautiful blue scales.

"I'm sorry I failed you," Kyndra said. "I promised I would return the egg and the Fae who killed your mate. I did neither."

The dragon briefly closed her eyes as if it were difficult for her to hear. She jerked her head toward the lair.

Kyndra looked from the entrance to the dragon. "You want me to go inside?"

The dragon repeated the gesture, and Kyndra started into the lair. The cave was massive in width and height, making it easy for two of the Blues to stand side by side. The deeper she got, the darker the lair became. She moved slowly until she heard the dragon behind her. Suddenly, the dragon inhaled deeply. Kyndra stood still, waiting for the flames to engulf her. Instead, the dragon blew fire on the water, giving light to the lair.

Kyndra stood in awe. The pool of water was huge, and off to one side was a large nest where the egg had been. She walked to the nest and knelt beside it.

"I didn't expect Isran to use the last of his life to shatter the egg," Aimery said as he walked from the shadows.

Kyndra looked up into his face and shook her head. "You couldn't have known."

"I've missed you."

How she had missed him too. Desperately.

"You left this behind," he said and held out his hand.

She looked at her cuff but refused to take it. "I'm not fit to wear it anymore."

"No one said only priestesses could wear the cuff. Did you know that Julieth sent you to Thav knowing what would happen to you?"

"What?"

"She said the dragons told her to do it."

Kyndra glanced at the Blue that had lain down. The female blinked her eyes at Kyndra. "I don't understand."

"Everyone in the realm is looking for you. Julieth and the Order are wondering when you'll return."

"I cannot return to the Order. I chose you over my vows."

He grinned and took a step closer to her. "I know, and I'm so glad you did. Still, you are a hero to the realm, Kyndra, whether you want it or not. You sacrificed your very soul to save me, the dragons and the realm."

"Aimery, the things I did with the black magic—"

"You did what you had to do," he interrupted her. "Just as I asked you to do."

"I want to believe you."

He took another step. "Why do you think the female sought you out? She could have killed you many times over. They've been watching you just as you've been watching them."

"And you? Have you been watching me?"

He nodded. "They told me where you were. You asked to be alone, so I left you alone."

"Except for today."

"I thought it time you understood what is going on in the realm. And I thought it time for you to take this."

He once more tried to give her the cuff. When she wouldn't take it, he reached for her hand and slid it up her arm. The sapphire eyes glowed for a moment before they turned to diamonds. Kyndra sucked in a breath and watched as the dragon turned from silver to gold.

"Wow," Aimery murmured. "What was that?"

"No one in the Order has ever gotten a gold dragon. It means…I've sacrificed a great deal for the realm."

Aimery smiled. "I already told you that."

Kyndra couldn't believe it. There was no way the cuff would have responded to her had she still had the black magic inside her. It was the reason she had taken it off in the first place. Yet, it had proven to her that things weren't as bleak as she had thought.

"I love you, Kyndra."

She looked into Aimery's eyes and smiled. "And I love you."

"Marry me. Spend eternity by my side. I've searched for you my entire life and feared I would never find you."

Her heart almost exploded at his words. He wanted her as his wife, despite what she had done with the black magic.

"I can't imagine going another moment without you by my side," he said as he knelt in front of her. "I want to kiss you, caress you, love you whenever I want. I want to fall asleep with you in my arms and wake up with the sun to kiss you good morning. You are my everything, the only thing that matters. Please."

Kyndra wiped at the tears that fell down her cheek. It had been near impossible to stay away from Aimery the past week. He had haunted her dreams and every waking moment. He was offering her everything, and she would be a fool to pass it up.

"Aye."

He pulled her against him and wrapped his arms around her. "Gods, how I love you."

Her chuckle died as he kissed her until she clung to his shoulders, her body throbbing with desire only he could bring out in her. "Shall we live at the palace?"

"Nay. I've a house."

"Where is this home?"

He stood and held out his hand. "Come. I'll show you."

As soon as Kyndra touched his hand he transported them. She gasped as she stood on the veranda atop a mountain overlooking a magnificent waterfall and a lake. "This is yours?"

"Just the view. The house is behind you."

Kyndra turned and laughed at the sheer size of Aimery's home. It was nearly the size of the royal palace but, set against the thick forest and mountains, it was spectacular.

He wrapped an arm around her. "It's my ancestral home, the house passed from generation to generation. What do you think?"

"And if I said no?"

"Then we'd find another home?"

She faced him and wrapped her arms around his neck. "Have you ever lived here?"

"Just as a child. After that, no. I was at the barracks as I worked my way through the army. Then, when I became commander, it was easier to live at the palace."

She glanced at the dark stones of the mansion with its steeped roof and many windows, then at the waterfall and lake. "I love it here."

"Then here it shall be," he whispered before he lifted her in his arms. In the next instant they were in the master chamber. Aimery set her on her feet and ripped her gown from her.

"I'll buy you new ones," he said, his voice thick with passion.

Kyndra didn't care about the gown. She only cared about Aimery and getting him out of his own clothes. When the last of his clothes hit the floor, they were in each other's arms, their kisses frantic as the passion consumed them. Kyndra parted her legs as he lifted her and wrapped them around his waist. She barely had time to realize what he was about before he slid inside her.

"Gods, you feel good," he whispered.

Kyndra wanted to answer him, but the throbbing of her sex wouldn't be ignored. When Aimery began to thrust inside her, she gripped his shoulders and rode the wave of desire.

All too soon, her climax consumed her. Aimery's fingers dug into her hips as he shouted her name and spilled his seed inside her. They fell back on the bed, their limbs tangled together.

"That's not how I wanted to take you," he said. "But once I saw you, I had to have you."

"I'm not complaining."

He grinned. "I'll make it up to you."

"Now?"

"After the wedding."

She raised her brows. "And when is the wedding?"

"How does an hour sound?"

"Perfect."

He ran a thumb over her lips. "I thought I had lost you

forever."

"I loved you too much for you to make a mistake."

"Julieth does want to see you."

She traced a finger down his arm.

"Are you all right with giving up the Order?" he asked.

"Aye. The thought of never having you isn't something I can live without. You are all I want."

He thumbed her nipple, making her groan. "If you don't stop, we'll miss the wedding."

"They can't have the wedding unless we're there."

Kyndra laughed and looked into the eyes of the man she loved. She had almost lost everything and, now, she had the world before her.

With Aimery at her side.

Epilogue

"If you don't stop pacing, I'm going to hit you," Kyndra said between clenched teeth.

Aimery stopped and sat beside her on the bed. He took her hand and held back a grimace as she squeezed. Sweat drenched her face, and her skin paled with each contraction. The labor had lasted far longer than Aimery would have liked, but Kyndra continued to tell him everything was all right.

He wasn't so sure.

"Ahryn?" he asked.

Lugus' wife raised her head and smiled. "I see the head. Just a little more, Kyndra."

Aimery smiled at his wife. The pregnancy had been a surprise, but one they had rejoiced in. As much as Aimery wanted children, he wanted his wife to be safe.

Kyndra grunted as another contraction came. Ahryn let out a whoop, and a moment later a loud cry erupted in the room.

"It's a boy," Ahryn shouted and held up the red, screaming infant.

A lump formed in Aimery's throat as he watched Kyndra take their son into her arms. She lifted her gaze to him, tears spilling from her eyes.

"We have a son, my love."

He kissed her and looked at his son. "That we do, love. What shall we name him?"

"What about Casheus?"

"Casheus it is."

Aimery wanted to stay just as they were, but Ahryn had already told the crowd that gathered below. Soon Kyndra's family as well as Theron and Rufina would want a look at the new addition.

"Are you happy?" Kyndra asked.

He entwined his fingers with hers. "More than words can say."

They shared a secret smile as the door to the chamber opened and the congratulations began.

Read on for an excerpt from
A DARK GUARDIAN

the first book in the thrilling
Shield series

Chapter One

The darkness of night summoned Evil like a warm tavern to a weary traveler. The velvety thickness blanketed any who dared to oppose its will. And the Evil enfolding Stone Crest had one task in mind - the demise of all.

"Faster," Mina whispered urgently into her mare's ear. She bent low over the horse's neck and chanced a look over her shoulder, her hair sticking to her face and neck as the ground raced beneath her.

The dark, menacing road was vacant, but she knew the creature was near. Stalking. Mina's skin tingled with anticipation, and her heart pounded fiercely in her chest as her mare continued to run toward the trees.

A terrible, unearthly scream rent the air. Mina quickly covered her ears. Her mare slowed, then stopped and danced around in fright.

"Nay," Mina hissed while she tried to gain control of her mount. "Run, Sasha, run. Our lives depend upon it."

The mare sensed Mina's anxiety because her long legs stretched out and the ground flew beneath them once more. Mina gripped the reins and Sasha's mane tightly as her blood rushed wildly with fear and dread. The hair on the back of her neck rose, but she didn't need to look behind her to know the creature followed very close.

Mina focused on reaching the clearing. Her mare was fleet of foot, the swiftest of her family's horses. If anyone could outrun the creature, it was Sasha. At least, Mina had thought so. Now she wasn't so sure.

A small smile formed on her face when she saw the clump of trees that signaled the clearing was just a short distance away. As she was about to reach the trees, the flap of wings overhead reached her.

Something long and sharp passed in front of her face and sliced across her arm. A frantic Sasha reared, and it was all Mina could do to hang on. Then suddenly, the world tilted and Mina jumped clear as her beloved mare collapsed and lay too still on her side.

Mina raised her eyes to the night sky and saw the creature that had come to their small village hovering above her, a sardonic smile on its grotesque face. Its small beady eyes flashed red in the gloom, and she knew her time was at an end.

Long, razor-sharp talons lengthened from its hands. She swallowed her failure like a lump of coal. This wasn't how it was supposed to end.

Fear immobilized her. She couldn't even scream. The creature moved slowly in the air towards her, as if he wanted to torment her prior to killing her. Before the creature's talons carved open her face, she saw a blur of movement out of the corner of her eye. In the next moment, she found herself thrown roughly to the ground and over the side of the hill. The weight of whoever had landed atop her knocked the wind from her lungs in a gush. As they rolled, she dimly heard the furious screams of the creature.

Just as she thought they might tumble for eternity, they

finally came to an abrupt, bone-jarring halt. She was afraid to open her eyes and find that another evil had taken her. After all, it had been the worst kind of wickedness, which had plagued her village for a month now.

A deep, soft voice reached her ears through her panic. A man's voice. "Are you all right?"

Slowly, she opened her eyes. Instead of a face, all she saw was the outline of his head. His tone held a hint of concern, but this was a stranger. She had come to mistrust anything that wasn't part of her village.

"Aye," she answered at last.

"I was beginning to think the fall had addled your brain." There was no mistaking the trace of humor in his meaning as he swiftly rose to his feet.

He held out a hand to her. She hated to do it, but she accepted his help because she didn't think she could gain her feet alone after the tumble she had just taken. As he pulled her to her feet, her arm burst into agonizing pain. She could barely move her hand, but she wasn't about to let the stranger know she was hurt and give him an advantage. It was something she had learned early in life. One had to be strong to survive in this land.

"It's not a safe night for a woman to be out alone."

She sensed he wanted to say more but held back. They were mere inches from each other, so she took a step back to offer herself more room. "There are many things which should keep people safely inside at night. Including men."

He bowed his head slightly. "I mean you no harm, lady."

She didn't believe that for an instant. Only a wandering idiot would take a stranger's word.

A bizarre whistle-like noise sounded from atop the hill. The stranger whistled back and then the eerie silence reigned once more. Not even the sound of crickets could be heard.

With her good hand she dusted off her breeches, and looked around for the dagger she had swiped from the armory. She couldn't believe she had dropped her only weapon.

"Is this what you seek?"

Mina grudgingly turned to the man and saw her dagger in his outstretched hand. She accepted the weapon. "Thank you. For everything." She bit her lip and thought of Sasha. Without another word, she began to race up the hill.

The stranger was at her side in an instant, aiding her when she would have fallen. When they reached the top, she came to a halt as five men on horseback stared at her. They sat atop their steeds like kings, watching her every move. She dismissed them when Sasha's soft cry of pain reached her.

She went to her mare and knelt beside her. She ran her hand lightly over the open gash across Sasha's whither and closed her eyes. It was a mortal wound.

"The mare has lost a lot of blood," the stranger said as he knelt beside Sasha. "I'm afraid she is lost to you."

Tears came quickly to Mina's eyes, and she tried to blink them away. Tears were for the weak. "I'm so sorry, Sasha," she said and leaned down to kiss the mare's head. "I should never have come."

She knew there was no way to save her horse, and to leave her like this was to see her suffer needlessly. With trembling hands, she held the dagger to Sasha's throat, but moments slowly drew on.

A large, warm hand encased hers. "Shall I?" the stranger offered.

Before she could change her mind she nodded. He took the dagger and she laid her head on Sasha's. It was over in a heartbeat. Sasha never made a sound, but it cut through Mina's soul like a silent scream of anguish.

She gave herself but a moment before she stood and looked around her as the moon broke through the dense clouds. Now she was alone with six men. Six heavily armed strangers.

The stranger rose and faced her. "I am Hugh."

"From where do you come?"

"London," he answered after a bit of a hesitation. He extended his arm to the men on horseback. "My companions are Roderick, Val, Gabriel, Cole and Darrick."

Each man bowed his head as Hugh said his name, and she was quick to note the array of weapons and the large shields, even in the cloud-laden night. Then, six pairs of eyes were on her.

"I am Lady Mina of Stone Crest."

"Well, Lady Mina, what manner of men would allow you to be out at night unprotected?"

Hugh's question had her thinking of the trap she and some of the villagers had set. "I'm not alone," she said with more conviction than she felt. Her eyes scanned the sky above her, but there was no sign of the creature.

"Where are your men?"

She turned and pointed toward the clump of trees. "In the clearing. I was luring a...an animal into a trap."

When she turned toward the men, the moonlight lit upon Hugh for just an instant, but in that moment she saw his skepticism. "It would have worked," she defended herself. "If Sasha had made it to the clearing."

"I hate to point out the obvious," the man in the middle said. Gabriel was his name. "But your men have yet to come to your aid."

Fear snaked its way through her and nestled comfortably in her stomach. These men could easily kill her. "I have only to call to them."

"Then call for I would meet the manner of men who would allow a woman to take such a risk," Hugh stated, his voice laden with unspoken anger.

"I would rather see the trap," Gabriel said and nudged his horse forward.

She stood her ground, ready to bolt, as Gabriel and his mount walked past her. She nearly sighed aloud, but recalled that she wasn't alone.

Hugh watched Mina closely. Her hesitation said all he needed to know. The men that should have been with her had deserted her. Had she lied? Was she alone?

The creature she had lured must have frightened them away. Yet, if what she said was indeed true and they had set a trap, then the men wouldn't have deserted her.

"Come," he said and put his hand on her back to guide her toward the clearing.

She walked a little ahead of him, and he tried not to notice that she wore breeches instead of a gown. It had been awhile since he had given in to his urges and bedded a woman, and with one walking just ahead of him with her backside swaying so enticingly from side to side, he found it hard to ignore.

He mentally shook himself and made his eyes look away from her delectable back end. Her hair had come loose from her braid and hung down her back in thick waves. Its exact color was hard to detect in the darkness, but he knew it was pale.

Thankfully, they reached the clearing then. Just as he suspected, no one waited for her. "Where is the trap?" he asked.

"I was to lead the creature into those trees," she said and pointed straight ahead. "Once I passed them, the men would cut a rope that held a spike which would impale the...animal."

Hugh heard the hesitation and wondered when she would tell them exactly what manner of beast had been chasing her. Could it be she really didn't know? Despite his misgivings about the situation, they had been sent to help.

And an order was an order

The creak of leather sounded loudly in the quiet as someone dismounted, and when Hugh looked over he found Gabriel beside him.

"Not a bad plan," Gabriel said thoughtfully as he stared at the trees. "I wonder if it would have worked."

"I guess we'll never know," Mina said softly.

"Scout the area," Hugh told his men. "See if any of Lady Mina's men are still around."

While his men did as ordered he handed Mina his water skin. She drank greedily before returning it to him.

"We aren't here to harm you."

She shrugged her shoulder. "We've learned not to trust anyone. Are you knights?"

"In a manner," he answered. "Do your parents know what you were about tonight?"

"They are dead."

That explained much. "By the beast that was after you?"

She became very still before she briefly nodded her head. "You know what hunts us?"

"I do," he admitted.

"How?" Her voice held doubt and hope.

"I'll explain once you're safe. Do you have any other family?"

"A brother and sister, and they did know what I was doing," she answered before he could ask.

Before Hugh could ask more questions, his men returned without good news. It was just as he expected, and it left a foul taste in mouth. There was no excuse to leave a defenseless woman alone to face the sort of evil they hunted.

"We will return you home safely." When she hesitated he said, "If you would prefer to face that creature alone and on foot, then we will leave you to it."

He had an idea she was about to do just that when the creature screamed some distance away and silenced any words she might have said. Without waiting for her to agree, he swiftly lifted her onto his horse.

He glanced at his men before he grabbed his horse's reins and mounted behind her. Their expressions said it all.

They had found exactly what they searched for.

Author Bio

Bestselling, award-winning author Donna Grant has been praised for her "totally addictive" and "unique and sensual" stories. She's the author of more than thirty novels spanning multiple genres of romance. Her latest acclaimed series, Dark Warriors, features a thrilling combination of Druids, primeval gods, and immortal Highlanders who are dark, dangerous, and irresistible. She lives with her husband, two children, a dog, and three cats in Texas.

Visit Donna at www.DonnaGrant.com

CPSIA information can be obtained at www.ICGtesting.com
Printed in the USA
LVOW11s1526021215

465055LV00001B/119/P